"Alex," Kate said, sighing in exasperation, **"why are you pursuing me?"**

He stopped walking and shoved his hands in his pockets, turning his head to stare up at the sky. "I don't know," he said quietly. "I could say you're the most beautiful woman I've ever seen, but you're not."

"You honey-tongued devil you," she said, choking on a spurt of surprised laughter.

"I could say you're the most interesting person I've ever met, but I've met Richard Nixon," Alex went on, studying the conflicting emotions in her face.

"And there must be at least . . . two women in the world who are sexier than I am," she added, helping him out.

"At least," he said, beginning to chuckle. "And several who are more successful."

"Well," she said, drawing in a deep breath, "we've eliminated why you're not interested in me, now tell me why you are."

"I don't know," he said, shrugging again. "Maybe it's that weird, warm feeling that takes over everytime I'm near you."

"You could get the same thing from a cup of cocoa."

He moved closer to her. "No, I couldn't . . . that's just the point. I've never felt it before. Only with you."

Trouble, Kate thought, backing warily against the wall behind her. There was sincerity in his voice, and that definitely meant trouble . . .

WHAT ARE *LOVESWEPT* ROMANCES?

They are stories of true romance and touching emotion. We believe those two very important ingredients are constants in our highly sensual and very believable stories in the *LOVESWEPT* line. Our goal is to give you, the reader, stories of consistently high quality that may sometimes make you laugh, sometimes make you cry, but are always fresh and creative and contain many delightful surprises within their pages.

Most romance fans read an enormous number of books. Those they truly love, they keep. Others may be traded with friends and soon forgotten. We hope that each *LOVESWEPT* romance will be a treasure—a "keeper." We will always try to publish

LOVE STORIES YOU'LL NEVER FORGET
BY AUTHORS YOU'LL ALWAYS REMEMBER

The Editors

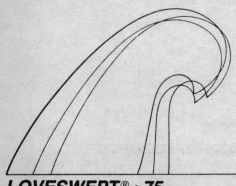

LOVESWEPT® • 75

Billie Green
The Count from Wisconsin

BANTAM BOOKS
TORONTO · NEW YORK · LONDON · SYDNEY · AUCKLAND

THE COUNT FROM WISCONSIN

A Bantam Book / January 1985

ISBN 0-553-21682-1

Published simultaneously in the United States and Canada

*Bantam Books are published by Bantam Books, Inc. Its
trademark, consisting of the words "Bantam Books" and
the portrayal of a rooster, is Registered in U.S. Patent and
Trademark Office and in other countries. Marca Registrada.
Bantam Books, Inc., 666 Fifth Avenue, New York, New
York 10103.*

PRINTED IN THE UNITED STATES OF AMERICA

O   0 9 8 7 6 5 4 3 2 1

To Daisy, because she knows the true meaning of the word "pudding" and doesn't hesitate to embrace one wholeheartedly when it comes her way.

One

"But you must believe me, *mon ange*. Would I lie to someone as lovely as you?"

Kate slowly sipped her drink, smiling vaguely at the man standing beside her. When he began to speak again she stifled a bored yawn and allowed her gaze to drift around the crowded room, as though she could actually see more than three feet in front of her face.

How do I get myself into these messes? she wondered. She didn't want to be at this party, pretending to be intrigued by a man with the I.Q. of a bagel. She wanted to be back at her friend Heather's house. Or better yet, back in her own home, sitting in her worn recliner, wearing her comfortable old fleece robe instead of the bit of gold nothing that an enthusiastic saleswoman had insisted was absolutely right for her.

"Listen to me, my sweet, I say to myself the

minute you walk in—François, I say, you must meet . . ."

Kate tuned out the persistent flattery that was making this difficult evening even more difficult. Schmaltzy flattery was bad enough, but schmaltzy flattery with a French accent was farcical. She was simply not equipped to handle that kind of thing without giggling.

Having already informed this tailor-made, gold-plated neo-Adonis that, no thank you, she honestly didn't care to dance with him . . . or to stroll down to the cabana . . . or even to go back to his place to experience a "*fantastique*" hot tub, what more could she say?

Suddenly Kate tensed, turning her head sharply to the right. There it was again. That crazy tingling on her face. For the last hour she had experienced this peculiar sensation at odd intervals, as though someone were staring at her off and on with concentrated intensity.

She lifted her hand to check her hair, but every strand of the honey-gold mass was still secure in the almost invisible snood.

This feeling of being watched was the weirdest thing, enervating and stimulating at the same time. At first she had explained it away as a figment of her overactive imagination. She was feeling out of her stratum, yet that still couldn't account for the prickling sensation on a different area of her body at a different time . . . sometimes on her face, sometimes sliding down her body. She had never felt something so odd.

Staring at the blurred crowd across the room, her eyelids drooping uncontrollably over her brown eyes, she felt the tingling grow stronger. Moistening her lips nervously, she tensed as the sensation slid down her body. It was as though she were being held in place by invisible, caressing hands.

Then suddenly she was released and she sagged in relief. It took a moment for her to regain her equilibrium, so forcefully had she responded to the sensation.

Kate jerked her head around when she felt someone blow in her ear. Murder! Was he still hanging around? She gave her persistent admirer a stare that was guaranteed to shrivel sumo wrestlers at ten paces and almost groaned when she received an enthusiastic smile in return.

I wonder how you say "shove it" in French?

Giving a small sigh of resignation, she decided this awful scene was the price she had to pay for being so headstrong. She simply had never learned to curb her impulsive, inquisitive nature. And once an idea had gotten a grip on her imagination, it refused to let go.

She probably should have known from the beginning that this escapade would cost her. It had all been too easy, the most difficult part being the transformation of ordinary Kate Sullivan into a glamorous woman of the world.

A new hairdo had helped. The waist-length hair she usually wore in one long braid down her back was now sleek and sophisticated, pulled to the crown of her head and bundled into a fine gold snood. And with discreet makeup, the salon had transformed the quietly pretty face that glowed with a healthy, outdoor look into a picture of classic beauty.

As a finishing touch, they had added false eyelashes and, although Kate had to admit they were very dramatic, the sooty fringe seemed unreasonably heavy, weighing down her eyelids to give her a sleepy, seductive look. The whole effect was of a chic sensuality that would have shocked her had she been aware of it.

One thing that couldn't escape her attention, however, was the amount of her flesh that was showing above the little gold dress, and the display definitely made her uneasy.

Maybe uneasy is too mild a word, she thought caustically as the man beside her pinned his bright Gallic eyes on her breasts.

"I have things to tell you, *ma chère,*" he murmured. "Things that will make you look at me with warmer eyes."

He leaned his head close as he spoke, his voice soft and romantic. Kate glanced up, and at that angle was presented with a most interesting view. She missed what he was saying as she found herself mesmerized by the hairs in his nose.

I wonder if I should tell him? she thought, then gave her head a small, distracted shake, deciding it would take something more devious to get rid of him.

And getting rid of him had suddenly become not only desirable but also necessary to her mental well-being. She was spending her evening staring vacuously into space trying to ignore the flashy protosimian at her side and wondering how long the human brain could be deprived of intelligent conversation before atrophying. Wondering when someone in this blurry crowd would discover she was a cartoonist who had sneaked in uninvited to copy their wealthy quirks in a syndicated strip. Wondering when they would see through her flimsy disguise and eject her from the midst of their Olympian gathering.

Enough is enough, she thought, glancing up again at the man beside her. Letting her frown melt into what she hoped was a seductive smile, she placed her hand on his sleeve and said, "I think I'm tired of this wine . . . um . . ."—what was the man's name?—". . . sweetums. Do you suppose you could possibly find a glass of champagne . . . pink champagne?" she added, to make the task more difficult, feeling very smug as he walked away because if he managed to find refreshment in the endless tangle of rooms he was better than she was.

She watched until he moved out of her range, then sighed in relief and leaned against the wall, feeling the hand-painted Chinese wallpaper against her bare back.

She cocked her head, hearing the orchestra in the next room swell above the noise with the beautiful strains of a Chopin polonaise, and smiled her first genuine smile of the evening.

Surveying the people immediately surrounding her, Kate wished again that she hadn't found it necessary to discard her glasses for the night. They hadn't exactly matched her new image, but she could see nothing clearly without them and her loss of vision left her feeling strangely disoriented.

Her limited range of vision made her feel as though she were enclosed in a thick, luminous fog. She hadn't realized being without her glasses would be this much of a handicap.

Ah, vanity, she thought as she wondered again in which room of the enormous house the food dwelt. She was sure that only the rumble of voices kept the people around her from hearing the rumble of her stomach.

How disgustingly underbred, she thought, holding back a snort of equally underbred laughter.

Then, as unexpected as before, the electric vibration of her nerve ends began again, racing quickly through her body, concentrating at times on her face. It was almost the same sensation that comes when the circulation returns to a foot or hand that has fallen asleep. Almost, but not quite. The pin prickles were missing and, as much as she hated to admit it, this was decidedly more pleasant.

Weird, she thought in distraction. *Very weird.*

Then a voice to her right caught her attention and she shook her head sharply, forcing herself to get back to the reason she was here.

The voice came from a small group of people on her immediate right. Now this was the kind of *grand monde* that Kate had been expecting. The bosomy, middle-aged woman was not one of the flashily dressed younger crowd. In fact, she was dressed a lot like Kate imagined Queen Elizabeth would dress for a party. Her face had a haughty, withdrawn expression as she raised her elegant brows in response to the woman speaking to her.

After watching the woman for several minutes, Kate discarded her as a possible character for the strip. She simply wasn't what Kate was looking for. In fact, nothing she had seen or heard so far had been what she was looking for. She didn't mind that what she was doing was unethical, but unethical *and* unproductive was too much.

One would think that in a place with Monte Carlo's reputation, a person would have been able to find at least a single character interesting enough, but it seemed as if bland was "in" this season. It was time to cut her losses, Kate decided, time to clear out and leave the festivities to the people who belonged in this mansion.

And besides, she thought with an impertinent grin, *if I don't find a hamburger pretty soon, I'll pass out right at their well-shod feet.*

No sooner had she made the decision than she acted on it and headed for the door that led to the garden. It was the nearest visible exit and, considering the distance she would have to walk to reach her rented car, a few hundred extra feet wouldn't make much difference.

Skirting the crowd of people who huddled in lively clusters around the patio and pool area, Kate caught her breath at the stunning blue blur in the distance. It had to be the Mediterranean. She had to admit the party was being held in a magnificent setting, situated as it was on the edge of a rugged cliff overlooking the glistening water. It was too bad she had never caught a glimpse of her unwilling host; he had excellent taste. People said money couldn't buy everything, she thought with a smile, but it certainly bought an outstanding view.

As a party of guests passed her, staring in momentary curiosity, Kate turned away from the scenery with a sigh of regret and moved swiftly toward a wooded area to the side of the mansion.

As she walked, the lights and smoke and noise of the party faded gradually to be replaced by cooling shadows, the sweet, heavy scent of roses and carnations, and the soft rustle of leaves.

Slowing her pace, Kate breathed deeply of the evening air, hoping it would clear her head, but instead it brought a sudden swimming dizziness as though maneuvering without her glasses had affected her equilibrium. She leaned slowly against a tree, resting her head on the rough trunk.

"That was very effective."

The deep, brown velvet voice brought her head up sharply to search around her for its source, but the shadows revealed nothing to her near-sighted gaze. For a moment she wondered wildly if the voice weren't simply one more piece of unreality in an extremely unreal night. Then the disturbing voice continued and the sheer force of it demanded that she accept its reality.

"I've been watching you through the window."

The words were casually spoken, but she thought she detected humor in his voice . . . as though watching her had amused him.

"All evening you've been looking straight through each man in the room as though he didn't exist. So cool and above it all, like Queen Boadicea surveying the great unwashed."

Suddenly a large shadow detached itself from a tree and she felt again that strange, ghostly tingle on her flesh as he continued to speak lazily. "Then you turned those sleepy siren eyes in my direction in the most blatantly erotic invitation I've ever encountered."

He chuckled quietly and the rich, mellow sound pulled at her senses.

"I'm sorry, Duchess, but whoever the look was intended for doesn't seem to have caught it. I watched and no one followed you out." He sounded almost apologetic. "But I'm here. Why don't you tell me what you had in mind? Maybe we could work something out."

I should have known, she thought in resignation. Considering the way her luck usually ran, she should have expected something like this. Why should she come out of the evening scot-free? Who else but Kate Sullivan would run into an oddball lurking on the grounds of a millionaire's mansion, an oddball who got his kicks from peeking through windows?

Suddenly the garden where they stood seemed isolated. Pulling away from the tree, she cleared her throat nervously. Although she tried to sound confident her words came out in a husky, apologetic whisper. "I'm—I'm afraid you've mistaken me for someone else."

He moved a step closer, his face still obscured by darkness, his shape looming large before her. "I guess I'm not who you were expecting."

He laughed again and the sound surrounded her, pinning her to the tree behind her. "I hate to say this, Duchess, but I'm afraid you were a little obvious—examining the prey with that cool, bored expression to intrigue, then seducing him with that last look."

The words gave the impression that he admired her, but by now she knew he was definitely laughing at her. She wasn't sure how she liked being the source of a stranger's amusement. For a moment she considered being offended, but as she pushed away from the tree, the content of what he said sunk in.

"Queen Boadicea?" she asked, intrigued against her will. She moved a step in his direction as the notion took hold of her imagination. "Did I really look like a vamp?" She smiled her generous, irrepressible smile. "No one has ever mistaken me for a *femme fatale* before. In fact," she added confidingly, moving even closer as she considered the idea, "I don't think I've ever met a *femme fatale*. Unless you count Marla Thompkins from high school . . . she wore Frederick's of Hollywood underwear under her miniskirt."

She smiled again, deciding she definitely liked the idea. But her smile faded when he stepped forward, his soft laugh filling the shadows. Her eyes grew round and she backed hastily to her former place against the tree.

"That's a start," he murmured huskily. "You've

got a stunning smile and it almost makes it worth my while . . . but not quite."

He continued to move steadily toward her as he spoke, and the closer he drew, the stronger the tingling became, until when he was a couple of feet away, her flesh almost burned with the sensation.

She felt it linger on her face as she nervously moistened dry lips, then on her full, firm breasts, causing her nipples to grow taut and thrust tightly against the thin gold silk. When the whisper of electric current moved slowly across her stomach and down to her hips and thighs, it spread a sizzling warmth to the secret places of her body.

She drew in her breath sharply at the incredible sensation, then shifted in acute awareness as the tingling returned swiftly to the rounded tops of her breasts that the indrawn breath had exposed above the low-draped bodice.

Leaning weakly against the tree, she closed her eyes in frustration. This man was definitely dangerous. Perhaps not in the way she had originally imagined, but dangerous nonetheless. She suddenly had the feeling that she was no longer in control of her own body.

Making a tremendous effort to pull herself together, Kate decided that not being able to see him clearly had to be part of the reason he disturbed her senses so. She drew the large tortoise-shell glasses from her purse and slid them on.

As she did, the moonlight struck full upon him and the shadowy garden seemed to fade and disappear into nothing until there was only his face. Her heart stopped for a breathless moment, then picked up again with a hectic, almost painful beat as she felt an indescribable, fleeting moment of recognition.

Not that Kate had ever seen him before; she definitely would have remembered him if she had. It wasn't recognition of a face or shape; it was something more basic and came from a deeper level.

The shadows filled the crevices in his face, the rays of the moon highlighting his hard, vital features. The overpowering masculinity, high cheekbones, and strong, distinctive nose gave him the look of a Comanche warrior . . . or a devil. Satan in tight black slacks and white shirt, open low at the throat, the sleeves rolled up to just below his elbows.

"Geronimo," she whispered vaguely.

He stopped abruptly. "I beg your pardon," he said, his voice frankly puzzled.

"Geronimo," she repeated.

"That's what you say when you jump out of an airplane." Now she could *see* the amusement on his strong, irregular features. "Somehow the significance of that escapes me," he said and shook his head.

"Come to think of it, that's how I felt a minute ago," she said frankly, her tone woeful; then she stared at him inquisitively as she recalled what he had said earlier. "Were you really peeking in the windows?"

"Yes, I really was." He chuckled.

"Aren't there guards or eunuchs or something hanging around to stop that kind of thing?"

"I haven't seen a single guard," he said, then paused thoughtfully. "There was one man who I couldn't swear wasn't a eunuch, but he was inside."

"Oh, really?" she asked, her eyes brightening with interest, and began to walk toward the villa. "I knew I was missing a lot by not wearing my glasses," she threw over her shoulder in a disgusted voice.

"Where are you going?" he asked, following behind her.

"I want to see," was her only explanation as she approached a large, diamond-paned window. Peering inside, she whispered, "Which one is the eunuch?"

His voice came from directly behind her as he watched from over her shoulder. "The bald one over there in the corner," he said, chuckling quietly.

"The one with the sash?" she asked. "No, definitely not a eunuch . . . look at the way he's eyeing that blonde." She paused. "Who's the one in the middle of the room who looks like Charles Laughton?"

"Let's see," he said, leaning closer. "That's Charles Laughton."

"Idiot," she said, smiling as she leaned against the wall. "It's a woman."

"Oh, my mistake," he apologized. "That's Charles Laughton's mother."

She laughed as she darted him a look of accusation. "You don't know who they are any more than I do."

"Yes, I do. It's just that the truth is boring compared to speculation."

"Give me a for instance."

"Okay . . . see that man?" He indicated a tall, elegantly dressed man standing next to an ebony escritoire. "Take a guess on what he does."

"Hmmm. He looks like a nobleman," she said finally. "A count or a duke at least."

"He makes hats," he said flatly.

"You're kidding."

"No, he does. They're very chic and very

expensive, but they're still hats." He nodded toward the same group of people. "Now look at the guy next to him. What would you say was his occupation?"

Kate looked at the stout, garishly dressed man whose features were so plain as to be outstanding. "You're trying to throw me off," she murmured. "Logically, he would be the duke, but I don't believe it. With that jacket, he's got to be a used-car salesman."

"He's a Greek millionaire . . . shipping money, you know," he added in slightly nasal mimicry.

"Okay, you win—" she began, then broke off when she heard loud laughter coming from the far corner of the room. "What about that lively redhead that everyone's paying attention to? She must be someone's mistress. She's gorgeous and seductive. The kind men fall all over."

"Wrong again." He grinned as he leaned against the window frame to look down at Kate. "She's the very proper wife of that man beside her and her official title is Lady Eleanor Whitfield."

"How disappointing . . . and dull," she added, raising one trim eyebrow in surprise. "Aren't there *any* rakes or playboys or notorious women in there? You would think in all that crowd of people there would be at least one person who was involved in a sex scandal or who was being blackmailed. I can't—"

She broke off suddenly as she was struck with an idea and was aware only at the edge of her mind of the way he swung around sharply to stare at her.

The characters were there, she thought, her mind working furiously. She had been looking for glamorous, worldly people, but the characters she did best were ordinary. If she could show an ordinary character thrown into this extravagant, slightly comic world of opulence . . .

"What are you doing?" he asked, still staring.

"Wait . . . wait," she said, hushing him as she searched her evening purse for the small pad she had placed in it earlier. With a felt-tipped pen she sketched like mad for a few moments, turning the too small pages frantically.

"May I see?"

His voice pulled her away from her intense concentration and she glanced up. "What?" she asked vaguely. "Oh . . . no, not yet. Let me think about it for a while."

Returning the pen and pad to her bag, she turned back to the scene framed by the window just as the orchestra began to play a lovely Strauss waltz. Chattering voices from the room were muffled as the music reached her ears, clear and vital. She turned sideways and closed her eyes to let the music wash over her as the rush of adrenaline faded away.

"You like Strauss?"

She smiled. "Have you ever met anyone who didn't like Strauss?" She opened her eyes and sighed. "But I must say, the people in there"—she gestured toward the room—"don't seem to appreciate it."

He smiled and, without a word, began to pull her slowly toward a small clearing.

"What are we doing?" she asked quizzically as he raised her left hand to his shoulder.

"We're appreciating it," he said, then reached down and removed her glasses, placing them in his breast pocket. As she squinted up at him in bewilderment he placed a hand on her waist while with the other he clasped her right hand. Then, incredibly, there in the moonlight as the music floated through the trees, they began to waltz.

His steps were sure and even as they circled on the carpet of grass, and at first Kate had the urge to laugh, then she felt herself traveling back to a more gracious, more romantic time. She could almost see the flickering light of thousands of candles and the gay, billowing skirts of a world past.

She was spellbound. Closing her eyes, she soared with the feeling, letting the exuberance of the waltz pour through her veins as they swung around their woodland ballroom for endless moments. The tempo of the music accelerated and they whirled round and round, moving faster and ever faster until she was breathless.

Suddenly, as the waltz died away, he caught her in his arms and stared down at her as she threw back her head and laughed in sheer exhilaration and delight.

For a moment he didn't move, as though he, too, felt the magic of the moment and was afraid of spoiling it. Then, when the orchestra began to play a more current love song, he placed both hands on her hips to bring her closer and they began to sway gently with the sensual music.

The extraordinary fantasy didn't have Kate totally under its spell. For one brief second before he lowered his mouth to her throat she thought about protesting—she honestly did. Then she felt the heat of his lips on her sensitive flesh and other thoughts took over.

He began to move his hands slowly. The movements weren't obvious and there was nothing she could pinpoint as being too forward, but though he was subtle, he was nonetheless seducing her. Silently, as they danced, he was making love to her with his strong, knowledgeable hands . . . his warm, mobile lips. Her neck arched in an uncontrollable response as she felt his warm breath on the sensitive cords of her neck, then the vulnerable curve of her shoulders.

The dazzling dance under the stars could have lasted for hours or only minutes. Time was lost for Kate as she heard the husky love words whispered in her ear, tasted the brandy on his lips, and felt his strong, masculine body pressed tightly against her softness. For the first time in her life she willingly relinquished control of her actions and simply followed where she was led.

So deeply affected was she by the enchanted moment that she had to stifle a tiny, protesting groan when he stopped the subtle, erotic movements and pulled her head away from his shoulder, framing her face with his long, hard fingers to stare down at her intently.

Lifting her eyelids lethargically, she exposed dazed brown eyes to his gaze. "Hi," she said lazily, then laughed merely because he did.

His hands tightened on her face for a moment, then he moved his thumb slowly across her swollen lips, inhaled a raspy breath, and began to walk with her through the trees.

Two

As they moved silently through the garden, Kate leaned against the man beside her, moving her cheek unconsciously against the soft fabric of his white shirt . . . fabric as soft and sensual as the finest silk. There was something about that shirt. Something she should think about, but she couldn't quite grasp what it was. Something . . .

Then without warning the fantasy ended. Reality descended upon her with the swiftness and devastation of lightning, shattering the enchanted dream.

It wasn't anything as noble as conscience that pulled Kate away from the fantastic interlude . . . nor her strong sense of independence . . . nor even good, old-fashioned common sense. No, she was pulled away by a force that makes no allowances for moonlight and roses and Johann Strauss . . . the noisy protestations of an empty stomach.

Giving a gasp of uncontrollable laughter at

the untimely interruption, she began, "How gauche . . . how totally, predictably—" then broke off abruptly when she realized where she was and who she was with.

Jerking her head up, she gaped at the man beside her. "Wait—hold on just a second," she gasped, slapping comically at the hand on her arm. Backing away, she gave a shaky laugh of disbelief, her brown eyes widening as she stared at him warily.

"What's going on?" she asked, not really expecting him to answer. "How did we get from there"—she pointed to the window—"to here?" She waved her hand quickly between the two of them. "I don't understand," she said, giving a short laugh. "I'm going heaven knows where to do heaven knows what with a . . . with a—" She glanced at him again, taking in his casual dress as she raised her hands in an emphatic gesture of self-disgust. "A peeping Tom! An honest-to-God, dyed-in-the-wool pervert."

"A gate-crasher berating a peeping Tom."

The quietly spoken words pulled her up short and she stared at him warily as he leaned lazily against a tree.

"Considering the untoward way you've behaved, Duchess, I don't believe you have a leg to stand on," he continued smugly, and Kate could hear the animation returning to his voice.

She continued to stare at him for a moment, then glanced away, struggling to keep from looking guilty. "My behavior was every bit as toward as yours . . . towarder," she mumbled defensively, then looked up at him in curiosity. "How do you know I came uninvited?"

Her question brought him up short for a moment, then he smiled. "I could tell by the way you acted," he said, dismissing her doubtful expression with a casual shrug. "You obviously didn't know anyone in the room . . . except perhaps the blond gift of the gods that was drooling all over you a minute ago." He sent her an inquiring glance. "Did he bring you?"

Kate felt it was better if she didn't answer that question, just in case this man was the gardener or someone else who belonged to the estate.

She forced a smile and, keeping her voice carefully casual, said, "Gee, it's been nice . . . um . . . Tom, but I think I'd better be going now."

When she turned to walk away, she felt her arm grasped by the long fingers that had caressed her moments earlier and she caught her breath, glancing back uneasily.

"Before you go, answer one question for me, Duchess," he said slowly, watching her with a genuinely puzzled expression on his face. "What happened? Why did you suddenly decide you didn't want to have anything to do with me? I could swear you were with me back there."

She stared at him speculatively. "That's two questions," she said at last.

"So answer two questions," he said in exasperation.

She stood for a moment gazing up at the stars, then cut her eyes back toward him. "My stomach."

"I beg your pardon?"

"I'm starving to death," she said emphatically. "I can't understand why you didn't hear it. It definitely wasn't a discreet growl," she added in a disgruntled voice. "It was one of those that starts high and picks up momentum as it gets lower, throwing in artistic pings and thrums as it goes."

"Pings and thrums?" he asked, throwing back his head to laugh in uninhibited enjoyment.

She grinned at him, unable to resist his laughter. "I never did manage to find the food in that gargantuan house and my stomach reminded me at a very opportune moment . . . I'm sorry, what did you say?"

"Nothing. Nothing at all," he said, his laugh settling down to a chuckle as he threw a companionable arm around her shoulders. "I don't think I've ever been thrown over for a canapé before. I can't say that I like it and it certainly doesn't do much for my image."

She began to walk again with him beside her. Somehow it seemed natural to be walking through the trees like that while he held her intimately at his side. She glanced up at him. "What's your image?"

"Suave pervert," he said without hesitation.

She acknowledged the thrust with a spurt of startled laughter. "No, I was wrong," she said without rancor. "You belong here, don't you?" Her glance became speculative when she asked as an afterthought, "What exactly do you do?"

There was a barely perceptible pause before he answered. "A little of everything."

"You mean like a handyman?"

"You could say that," he said, nodding. "As a matter of fact, I'm very handy at finding food."

He stopped suddenly and Kate looked up to find they were standing at a side entrance to the villa. When she realized he planned to usher her through the door, she dug in her heels, suddenly refusing to budge.

She was doing it again, she thought in amazement. She was amiably going along with a man unknown to her, a man she had never seen before tonight.

She reached out to retrieve her glasses from his pocket, slipped them on, then leaned against the wall as she began to search the figure before her for a clue to her incredible behavior.

He was not a man who would ever be mistaken for someone else. Not handsome in the conventional sense, his face was breathtakingly striking—a piece of granite chipped away to reveal strong, almost harsh lines. His features had an ageless quality that could have placed him anywhere between thirty and forty-five, and his deep tan merely added to his dark image. A bit longer than was fashionable, his black hair and rugged, unconventional features gave him a look of barely contained power so exciting Kate had to struggle to control her escalating pulse rate.

"Well, what have you decided?" his amused voice prompted.

Startled from her reverie, Kate blinked in confusion and found the object of her thoughts leaning indolently beside her, effectively trapping her between his body and the rough plaster wall, looking disgustingly pleased by her intense scrutiny.

The man was . . . he was . . . She couldn't find an adjective to describe him. The word beautiful popped into her head, but she discarded it quickly, knowing it was wrong. She realized that by some standards he might even be considered ugly and she couldn't put her finger on any one feature that appealed to her so much; she simply knew she reacted to him more strongly than anyone she had ever met.

But he was just a man after all and she could find nothing in his person that gave a clue to the staggering effect he was having on her emotions.

To be perfectly honest, she didn't trust this sudden surge of intense feeling. It had happened too fast to be real.

"I've really got to go," she murmured to herself, shaking her head. "Something very strange is going on in my head. I'm coming very close to trotting willy-nilly after a man who all but attacked me."

"Attacked you!" he said in mock astonishment, his midnight eyes gleaming. "My dear Duchess, I haven't touched you since the minute you indicated my advances weren't welcome."

"You have me backed against the wall and you're looming over me like some damned great mountain," she accused, her belligerence holding a degree of desperation.

"Six two is hardly a mountain and you backed against the wall without my help . . . I thought perhaps you had a plaster fetish, but I wasn't going to mention it," he added with a wicked grin. "I merely wanted to feed you. Is that a crime?"

She studied him for a moment, weakening against her will as the force of his smile warmed her. "How do I know what you intend? For all I know you could be planning to take me to the dungeon . . ."

Kate ruined the dramatic accusation by giggling. She couldn't help it. No matter how serious the situation, her sense of humor eventually got the better of her. She struggled to control it, to maintain her dignity, but it was no use. With her dignity taking its usual backseat, she looked up at him through her sooty, temporary eyelashes and let her offbeat sense of humor have free rein.

". . . and there," she continued with relish, moving away to punctuate her speech with enthusiastic gestures, "inflamed by my startling beauty, abuse my childlike innocence with your ravening appetites, afterward disposing of my broken body by mailing little bits and pieces of me to small, uninteresting places all over the world."

She glanced over her shoulder to find him whistling under his breath as he stared up at the sky. After a moment, he lowered his gaze to her. "Are you through?"

She nodded, smothering a laugh as she took in his long-suffering expression.

"You're sure?" he added, solicitously. When she nodded again, he said, "If I promise not to chop you up and send you C.O.D., will that reassure you?"

"And the part about abusing my childlike innocence?" she prompted inquisitively.

"We'll negotiate on my ravening appetites," he hedged, then, when her expression changed, he reassured her lazily, "Just teasing, Duchess."

Kate stared intently at the smiling man, then at the ground, nibbling on the tip of a pink nail as she considered the problem. Despite the warning signals going off in her head, she was seriously tempted to go with this stranger. Common sense and a deeply ingrained streak of self-preservation warned against it, but she was woman enough to be intrigued by this man who stirred so many different emotions in her.

She raised confused eyes to the object of her thoughts, catching his face in an unguarded moment. There was a strangely wistful quality about the look in his eyes. The vulnerability she saw there was her undoing. It didn't fit her impression of him at all and shook her in a way she didn't understand.

She opened her mouth to tell him to lead on, but before she could speak, he straightened and snapped his fingers.

"Of course! You're waiting for a formal introduction, aren't you? Very wise of you," he added,
nodding sagely, then he opened the side door.
"Don't move from this spot, Duchess. I'll be right
back."

She didn't have long to wait, but before he
returned, the memory of her weakness as they
danced rose up to plague her and she began to
question the wisdom of her decision. She had
taken one step away when the door opened again
and he stood there with a thin, blond man who
was obviously a servant.

The nervous young man stepped forward after a nod of encouragement from Kate's dark
stranger. Even though they were standing in the
dark, there was enough moonlight reflected by
the white wall for her to recognize the painful
blush on the younger man's face.

"Mademoiselle," he said shyly, "may I present
the monsieur. He is very respectable. He is . . . ah
. . . gainfully employed." He said the words as if
reading a list. "He has never been in jail. . . . But,
Monsieur," he said, turning to the other man,
"what about the time—"

"That doesn't count. Continue, Henri."

The nervous young man looked at Kate, then
shifted his gaze to the stars as though asking for
divine intervention and continued as ordered. "He
is kind to children. He hardly ever"—he swallowed
noisily—"kick old females or dogs and"—his expression was pained as he finished in a constricted
voice—"he has not *chop' up* anyone since the doc-
tors have change' his medication."

By the end of Henri's incredible speech, Kate
had to hold on to the wall to keep herself upright.
She watched through tears of laughter as the
"monsieur" shooed away the young man with a

careless "That was fine, Henri," before turning to Kate. "*Now* will you let me feed you?"

"I have to admit I'm curious," she said, trying to catch her breath. "Promise you'll tell me all about the time in jail that doesn't count," she added as she moved through the door with a confidence that most certainly would have been shaken had she seen the gleam in her companion's dark eyes as he followed her.

"You won't regret it," he said as they walked down a dark hall. "They like me in the kitchen."

He began to whistle and the sound echoed in the dim hallway. Kate was just beginning to wonder if they actually were going to the dungeon when he opened another door and they walked into a huge, brightly lit kitchen.

The room seemed to be filled with bustling people. Two women arranged food on large silver trays; several men carried huge stainless-steel bowls from a walk-in refrigerator. Tall metal pots as big as milk cans sat on the stove.

The wonderful smells pervading every corner of the room caused Kate's stomach to resume its unhappy protestations. She looked up at the man beside her and said longingly, "You distract them and I'll grab a tray."

He laughed. "That won't be necessary. Just come with me."

Kate followed close behind as he moved across the room, then slowed warily when he stopped beside a small man who was in the process of rapping a wooden spoon across the knuckles of a very large man arranging food on one of the trays.

The small, dark chef was wrapped in a voluminous apron and wore a white beret-type cap on his dark head. When he turned to scowl impatiently at the intruders in his kitchen, Kate quickly hid her hands behind her back, then glanced up at the man beside her.

"Moustafa, wonderful Moustafa," he said in a humble voice. "May we have some food? Just a crumb to hold off starvation? Something you had intended to throw away?"

"Food!" the small man exploded, his accent one Kate didn't recognize. "It's not enough that I prepare food of the gods to throw to unappreciative pigs, now you want I should watch the pigs eat?"

The string of expletives that came next could only have been a mixture of every language known to man, and Kate's mouth dropped open in wonder at his proficiency.

She leaned close to her new friend. "They like you in the kitchen, huh?"

He laughed, then continued to cajole the small, volatile chef. "But you won't have to watch us, Moose. We'll sit quietly in the pantry and I swear you'll never know we're there."

"Take it! Take it all," the little man fussed. "Here . . . here, would you like my watch and ring also?"

Kate's companion picked up a small platter and began to fill it with an assortment of the food that lay before them. Five minutes later they sat on a sturdy wooden table in the roomy pantry, their feet swinging beneath them as they dined on crab legs and caviar, sweetbreads and soufflé . . . what he called "a gentle sufficiency."

With a glass of wine in one hand and a piece of exquisitely tender crab meat in the other, she made an inarticulate sound of pleasure; then, after removing a drop of wine from her lower lip with the back of her index finger, she turned to the man beside her.

"Moose?" she said incredulously, then started to giggle as she repeated, "Moose?"

He swallowed a mouthful of cheese unsteadily, punching her gently in punishment as his choking laughter increased her amusement.

"Would you be brave enough to call him Moose?" he asked when he was able to speak.

"Oh, no! If he wants to be called Moose, then Moose it is." She glanced up at him. "He talked so fast I couldn't understand a word. I swear one time he said, 'Where's the *boeuf*?' " she said, leaning against her companion, very much at ease. "What did he say as we left? He kept repeating a word over and over."

" '*De l'audace, encore de l'audace, et toujours de l'audace,*' " he quoted, chuckling. " 'Audacity, more audacity, and even more audacity.' Afterward he looked at you with a definite gleam in his eyes, then at the tray of food, and said, '*Si jeunesse savait, si vieillesse pouvait.*' "

"Should I ask what that means?" she asked warily.

" 'If youth only knew, if age only could.' I believe he thinks I'm wasting time eating when I could be making love to you," he said softly.

Kate felt a shiver run up her spine and looked away quickly, but before she could reply, the sensuality in his voice and eyes disappeared as quickly as it had come.

"Would you like dessert? I could creep in while Moose's back is turned and get something."

"No, I'm content with our gentle sufficiency," she said, smiling up at him. She looked around the room he called a pantry that was as big as a normal kitchen. "You know, this is much nicer than the party out there."

"You didn't like the party?"

"It was interesting, but not exactly my style. I like watching people, so I might have enjoyed it more if I had been able to see." She paused. "But only as an observer. I can't relate to those people. I listened to them talking about stocks and bonds and Dior underwear, none of which I know anything about. They all looked so gorgeous, while I was standing there trying to suck in my thighs."

She watched his laughing face for a moment, then her brown eyes brightened with curiosity, a smile lingering on her full lips. "Isn't it strange? I feel like I've known you for years, but I still don't know your name." She laughed. "I can't keep calling you Tom."

"Actually you could," he said, an odd smile twisting his lips as he watched her keenly. "One of my names is Thomas."

"One of them?" She leaned back, her expression intrigued. "Do you have a lot of names?"

"Dozens. Alexandre Marie Thomas Adrien . . ."

She started to laugh in surprise at the string of names, then something began to nag at the edge of her mind and she moved slowly upright.

". . . Gervais Alain René Delanore . . . Comte de Nuit," she finished, closing her eyes with a fatalistic sigh. *The shirt*, she thought in dismay. The shirt was silk. That was what had bothered her earlier. She opened her eyes to give him a rueful glance. "My host?" she asked in resignation.

"The same," he confirmed with a grin.

She looked around the pantry, taking in nothing as she assimilated what he was saying, then glanced back to the man beside her. "Say something rich," she said in a last attempt to deny the truth.

"Send me the bill," he offered, not attempting to hide his amusement.

"That'll do," she said, and began to study him closely. "So you're a count. I thought you were Belgian, not American. An American count?" Before he could respond, she added curiously, "Why are you sitting in the butler's pantry with the hoi polloi instead of mingling with your guests?"

"It looked like a very dull party, so I escaped to the garden . . . at least it looked dull until I began watching you through the window." He shrugged nonchalantly, then added, "And the title is Belgian, but I don't happen to be."

She stared at his strong face for a moment, then slid off the table. "It's been real nice, Alexandre-Marie-whatever, but I think I'd better go now."

"Wait." He slid down quickly and grasped her arm as she headed toward the door. "Aren't I allowed to know your name in return? I'm sure I saw it on the invitation, but it must have slipped my mind."

"Cute," she said, acknowledging the thrust. "Very cute. You know I wasn't invited." She glanced up at him. "Are you going to have me thrown out?"

He laughed. "Somehow you don't sound very worried about that possibility. No, you may have attended the other party uninvited, but you definitely had an invitation to this one," he said quietly, giving her a coaxing, crooked smile.

"My name is Kate Sullivan," she said finally, unable to repress an answering grin. "I could stretch it out to Kathryn Louise Sullivan, but even that doesn't come near Alexandre, etcetera, etcetera."

"It could come near if it wanted to," he said softly, then when the color began to rise in her cheeks he added, "It's a very nice name, Kathryn.

And if it makes you feel any better I usually go by Alex Delanore."

"No one calls me Kathryn." She glanced away, avoiding his eyes. The softness of his tone brought a strange feeling to the pit of her stomach. "It's just plain Kate."

"Never plain," he objected. "But you're right, Kate is for a party in the butler's pantry."

He moved closer and placed his hand on the wall above her head. When he spoke again his voice had deepened and she tensed, knowing what to expect. She didn't have to wait long. Within seconds the electric charge she had felt earlier came back full force.

"Kathryn is for making love," he continued, as though he weren't aware of the fact that she was slowly dissolving and would soon be a puddle of mush at his feet.

She slid away from him warily, avoiding the lips that drew near. "I think," she said with a breathless laugh, "that you could be a very dangerous man, but—but I am *not* going to stay to find out."

His mood shifted abruptly and she stopped in surprise at the startling change. He shoved his hands in his pockets and the expression on his face reminded her of a small, belligerent boy.

"But you can't leave," he said stubbornly. "You haven't told me why you came." He ran his eyes over her. "You don't look like a groupie."

"Thank you . . . I think. I came to—" She paused, wondering how to explain the idea that had gripped her earlier that day. Then, with a shake of her head, she decided not to try. Why bore him with her life story? "I came to get something," she said finally.

She didn't actually see him stiffen. It was

more an awareness of his sudden alert posture, a quickly disguised watchfulness. "And did you get it?" he asked casually.

She considered the question for a moment, thoughtfully tugging at her earlobe. "Not enough," she murmured finally. "No, I don't think it's going to be enough."

"Who are you, Kate?" His voice sounded strange, as though he were repressing some strong emotion.

She stared at him in curiosity, then shrugged. "I'm a tourist," she said dryly. "You know, those people with cameras who get in the way of your Lamborghini."

"I drive a Ford." He relaxed perceptibly. "You sound as though you don't like wealthy people."

"What's not to like? I just know where I belong," she said firmly. "And I don't belong here."

He remained silent for a moment, then with equal firmness asked, "When can I see you again?"

"Didn't you hear what I said?" she asked in exasperation.

"You said you don't belong here," he said, smiling. "So we'll meet somewhere else. I could probably find a local soup kitchen if you'd be more comfortable there."

She laughed. "If you're trying to make me feel ridiculous, it won't work. I think my position is perfectly understandable. Most people are uncomfortable with people whose lifestyle is different. We all tend to stick to people who have a common background, common goals. It's not really prejudice; it's more a matter of comfort. It's nice to know how other people live and what they think, but when it comes to choosing companions, we all want people around us whom we can relate to, whom we can understand and empathize with."

He shook his head and smiled. "I didn't intend to ridicule you, but your ideas seem a little narrow. You can't choose your friends by their bank account and social life. It has to be because of what's inside them." He paused, staring down at her, studying her face as though he could find some vital key to her personality in her features. "Haven't you ever known anyone who lives just exactly as you do, but seems to have nothing in common with you?"

She thought for a moment, then nodded reluctantly.

"So when can I see you again?"

She made an exasperated gesture. "You're not just someone with a different lifestyle; you're a *count*. And *Cinderella* was never my favorite fairy tale."

"What was your favorite?"

She laughed. "I can't remember the name of it, but it was the one where the villainess ends up being rolled down a hill in a barrel lined with nails."

"My, my," he said, lifting his heavy eyebrows. "Vicious little darling, aren't you?"

"I was teasing," she said, chuckling. "My favorite was actually the story about the girl who had to weave capes from nettles in order to change her brothers from swans back to people." She glanced at him. "Yes, I know what you're thinking. It does say something about me. I believe in accomplishing what I want by the honest sweat of my brow. The work ethic is very deeply imbedded in my nature."

It suddenly struck her that if she really believed what she was saying, she could possibly have trouble with her new cartoon about high society. Would her feeling show through and taint the flavor of her work?

She shook her head slowly. "Maybe what I'm planning to do isn't the right thing," she said quietly, unaware of how closely he watched her. "I simply don't know if I can pull it off."

He was silent for a few seconds. "Would you like to tell me what it is you're planning to do?"

"It's only tentative, you understand," she began, anxious to discuss the idea with someone. "But the thing that's really throwing me is my feeling toward the subject. Do you suppose I might just screw up everything because of some stupid buried contempt?"

"Well—"

"It's different from anything I've ever done . . . that makes it a challenge," she continued as though he hadn't spoken. "But you have to remember that I'm from Plum, Texas. We don't get many society folk down that way. There are all kinds of hidden traps. Do you think I should stick to something I know better?"

"Actually—"

"Oh, I know it would be cowardly to back out now, and I've never turned my back on something just because it was difficult. If I'm intelligent enough to recognize the problems, then surely I'm intelligent enough to work them out." She looked up at him and sighed happily. "Thanks, Alex. It always helps to have someone else's input."

"My pleasure," he said doubtfully, shaking his head in amused confusion. "Now that we've gotten that straightened out," he continued, "when am I going to see you again?" Before she could protest, he clasped her hand and said, "*Please.*"

She glanced up at him and caught a strange expression on his face. It was very similar to the one she had seen earlier, almost vulnerable. Then he shook his head in regret and drew in a deep breath. Murmuring something softly in French, he touched his lips to hers before she could move away.

"Have you no blood in your veins, Kathryn?" he whispered against her lips. "How can you walk away from these emotions, these sensations? When I saw you in the garden I was feeling empty and alone. I thought you were . . . well, I thought you were something that you could never be. I thought you were the kind of woman who leaves you feeling emptier than ever. Then I touched you and saw the look in your eyes and"—he paused and a strange expression came to his face—"I was filled with the most incredible emotion. It was almost a renewal." He touched her neck softly with his hand. "This means something, Kathryn. And in an age when so much is meaningless, we can't just let it go."

Kate almost moaned aloud as the sensations that had disturbed her in the garden were redoubled. His whispered message touched more than her brain and the crazy tingling became violent shivers as she fought the pull of his nearness.

I'm in trouble, she thought wildly. *Deep, deep trouble*. She didn't know how to fight this kind of attraction. Until she met him she hadn't even known such a thing could exist.

Staring mutely into his dark eyes, she silently begged for a release from the hold he had on her. His hand traveled from her neck to her shoulder, and although she told her body to move away it moved into the caress.

The struggle going on inside her brought a

sheen to her eyes and she closed them, murmuring, "No . . . please."

Then, just when she thought that nothing could save her from the incredibly intense emotions welling up inside her, they heard a shout outside the pantry and he looked away from her, muttering "Damnation!" under his breath before he went to the door.

Kate sagged against the wall, feeling drained of energy and emotion. She had to get away. She couldn't allow this to happen again. If it were merely physical attraction she felt for him, she could have handled it. But what she'd experienced was no mere physical thing. It was a strength-sapping voodoo spell. It took away her identity and she wasn't ashamed to admit that it frightened her.

As she slowly gained control of her emotions, Kate became aware of the altercation taking place in the kitchen. Walking to the door, she saw Alex trying to separate two of Moustafa's helpers while the small chef waved his hands frantically in the air.

She didn't give herself time to think; without a backward glance she strode out the way they had come in and within minutes she was in the garden again, running breathlessly toward the front gate.

It was only later that it occurred to her he never explained about the time in jail that didn't count. And it was much later that she began to wonder about why he had attracted her so much . . . and about the uncharacteristically hysterical way she had run from that strange attraction.

Alex leaned back in the leather chair, stretching his legs out before him as he stared moodily into the brandy that was left in the large crystal snifter. He glanced up as a tall black man entered the study.

"The king is in his counting house," the man quipped, then added, "drinking hundred-year-old brandy. So how did the soirée go, Count?"

Alex laughed as he threw out a casual vulgarity. "They ate everything in sight and there were the usual number of drunks to carry out. I suppose that means it was a success." He paused, frowning. "Paul, what the hell am I doing here?"

"Living the good life?" his friend offered, then at Alex's vicious expletive he sobered. "You know what you're doing here. And at one time you thought it was worth it. Have you changed your mind?"

"No." He sighed roughly. "No, I guess not. It's just that . . . I'm beginning to think I'll never get back to the real world." He glanced away and said slowly, "I don't like people thinking I sit around all day spending money and avoiding honest labor."

"People?" Paul said skeptically. "Since when have you been worried about what people think?"

Alex accepted the knowing look in his friend's eyes. "You're right," he said. "It's one particular person I'm worried about. She doesn't like counts, Paul." He swirled his brandy and studied the liquid in motion. "She didn't exactly *say* she didn't like them, but I could sense a hesitancy. I was just wondering if she would like me better if I were still merely the owner of a construction company."

Paul raised his brows in interest. "You met someone tonight? Here?"

Alex nodded, taking in his friend's sudden alertness.

"How do you know she's not part of this business?" Paul asked carefully.

Alex thought of the way Kate had evaded his questions about being at the party and frowned, then he shook his head slowly. "No, she doesn't have anything to do with all that. I'm sure of it."

"You don't sound too sure."

"Well, I am," he said brusquely. "The only thing I'm not sure of is if I'll see her again. I have her name and this is not exactly a place where she can easily hide, but when I find her, will she see me?" He smiled grimly. "I want to see her again . . . and again and again."

Alex glanced up to find his friend shaking his head and gave a disgusted laugh. "So what do you think, my friend? Do you think I can pull it off?"

Paul laughed. "That's like asking 'How deep is a well?' I have to know a little more about it, but if it makes you feel any better, there's always a chance that anything can happen. After all, the Church finally pardoned Galileo."

Alex stared at his friend silently for a moment. "As a matter of curiosity, how long was Galileo in the can before he got his pardon?"

"Oh, about three hundred and fifty years or so." Paul laughed.

"Thanks," he said dryly, rising slowly to his feet. "But I don't think I'm prepared to wait that long."

"Now I really am curious. I've never seen you this disturbed about a female," Paul said slowly. "Who is this wonder woman?"

Alex smiled. " 'Plain Kate,' " he quoted. " 'And

bonny Kate, and sometimes Kate the curst. But, Kate, the prettiest Kate in Christendom.' "

He fell silent for a moment, then grinned in secret satisfaction and murmured, "And just maybe 'I am he born to tame you, Kate.' "

Three

Kate carried her coffee to the open terrace door, quietly absorbing the beautiful morning. Moving a few steps out onto the terrace, she wondered why, after staying up most of the night sketching, she felt as refreshed as if she had had the prescribed eight hours. Perhaps it was the feeling she had awakened with—a strange expectancy, as though the next act of her life was about to begin.

Leaning against the stone wall, she shook off the fanciful thought and cast her mind back to the tricks her demon creative forces had played on her in the early hours of the morning.

Maybe she'd been overly confident about her idea for the new cartoon. It had seemed so very simple. She would use the mania for soap operas that was sweeping the United States, capturing it in cartoon form.

But she was finding that it was anything but

simple. Every time she began to outline and sketch, her pen took her in a different direction. She couldn't seem to draw the elegant characters she had seen the night before—at least not in a serious vein. She hadn't intended to do caricatures. But the characters she was working on were saying and doing things that were totally off-the-wall.

Oh well, Kate thought, shrugging. She would figure it all out somehow. She always did. In a week's time she would be back at her drawing board in Texas, getting down to some serious work, and this would seem like a dream.

She straightened to inhale deeply of the crisp morning air, gazing out at the splendor before her. The sun was rising with breathtaking force, splashing brilliant colors onto the houses on the side of the hill.

Turning sideways, she watched as Heather joined her on the terrace. "Oh, heavens, how I love this place." Kate sighed, gesturing exuberantly. The golden braid hanging down her back swung gaily across her shoulder as she turned back to the view. "Even the urban blight here is picturesque. It's all so foreign . . . so *un*-Texas."

Heather laughed. "The urban blight is not picturesque close up, but I know what you mean. I adore it."

Kate glanced back at her friend's lovely, animated face. Heather had been her closest friend for as long as she could remember. Together they had lost their front teeth, bought their first bras, and agonized over their first loves. It seemed strange to be meeting her now in this exotic country. So much had happened since they had last met and yet, in a way, it seemed that they had never been apart.

Heather looked the same—petite, dark, and

bubbly. Kate sometimes felt that no matter how much the world changed around them, Heather would remain the same.

The small woman moved to sit at the white wicker table. "Where did you disappear to last night?" she asked, leaning back lazily.

Kate moved to join her friend at the table, pushing her glasses up on her nose. "I went hunting . . . in very exclusive hunting grounds," she said, grinning in remembrance.

The brunette's green eyes grew bright with interest. "Does it have anything to do with the bundle of mail you collected yesterday?"

"When did you get so clever?" Kate asked, raising a delicate eyebrow. "You're right. It has everything to do with that. Three more newspapers canceled my strip. I'm being dropped like a hot rock by every newspaper except the ones that don't count."

"I don't believe it," Heather said with stubborn loyalty.

"Believe it," she said, sighing as she stared up at the bright blue sky. "Deep down I knew it was coming. My characters were getting stale." She grimaced. "I just don't have the enthusiasm for it that I used to. I thought about revamping it, but now I think that's the wrong way to go."

"Why worry about it? Why not stay with us for a few months?" Heather asked enthusiastically. "It's not as though you need the money. You've still got what your parents left you and the money from the cartoon. You must have been socking it away for years; this is the first time I've known you to spend any money on yourself."

She shrugged. "I have everything I need."

"You see what I mean," Heather said in exasperation. "How about what you want? You live as though you don't know where your next meal is coming from and you're probably Plum's wealthiest citizen."

Kate threw her a skeptical glance. "That's really saying a lot. When I'm at my place in Dallas the wealthiest person in Plum is then Mr. Jackson at the gas station."

"Does he still have the gas station?" Heather asked, then grinned when her friend began to laugh. "Okay, so maybe being the richest person in Plum is not wonderful, but you've got to admit you're comfortable."

Comfortable, Kate mused, seeing a rich man's pantry in her mind's eye. She had her house in Plum, a town house in Dallas, and money in the bank for her old age. But comfortable was a long way from a mansion in Monte Carlo. Sullivan was a long way from Delanore and light years away from de Nuit.

Of night. How appropriate for a man who had appeared to her in the darkness of night. She didn't want to think about that dance under the stars. Her reactions to a total stranger were too much of a puzzle for her puny brain.

But later in the pantry, her feelings were recognizable. There had been an immediate rapport between them that she knew from experience was rare. They had been on the same wavelength. At least they had been until he had revealed his identity. She still found it hard to believe the man she had laughed with was a member of the Belgian nobility.

Ah well, she thought, sighing. It would be something to tell her grandchildren about, a moment of excitement to remember when she was home and life returned to normal.

Normal, she thought with a grimace. Somehow, after last night, normal didn't sound very inviting. Would she spend the rest of her life waiting for that next act to begin?

"Hey, are you listening?"

"I'm sorry," Kate apologized, glancing up to find Heather staring at her in exasperation. "What were you saying?"

"I said, where were you last night? You left here yesterday with a funny look in your eyes, then I heard you come in at two o'clock this morning. I don't want to play mother, but where were you?"

Kate widened her eyes in exaggerated surprise. "And what were you doing up at two in the morning?"

Incredibly, Heather blushed. "Evan came home last night," she said, smiling shyly.

"Oh, he did, did he? And where is the poor man this morning?" Heather's husband, Evan Martin, had been out of the country since a week before Kate's arrival in Monte Carlo. And even after six years of marriage, Heather still seemed a little lost without him. "Still in bed recuperating from your welcome?" Kate teased.

"He left for work early," she explained, then grinned wickedly. "I don't think he got too much sleep, though." She glanced up suddenly. "Now stop avoiding my question. Where were you?"

"I spent a fortune on a ridiculous dress and hairdo and"—she fluttered her own pale eyelashes—"false eyelashes, and I went to a party."

Heather stared at her in surprise. "Why didn't you let me see you?" she complained, then leaned forward. "What did your dress look like . . . something really sexy, huh?"

"Sexy?" Kate mused. "Yes, I guess you could say that. In fact, I felt very daring until I got close enough to see what some of the other women were wearing. I swear, Heather, one of them looked like she was wearing nothing more than a little artfully draped Saran Wrap."

"You idiot!" Heather exclaimed. "You've been buried in your cartoons too long. It's about time—" Suddenly she paused. "Wait a minute . . . whose party? Why wasn't I invited?"

Kate took a leisurely sip of coffee, then glanced at her friend with a gleam of mischief in her brown eyes. "*I* wasn't invited. I crept in so slickly you would have been amazed." She paused, then said slowly and clearly. "I crashed the Comte de Nuit's grand society bash."

Heather choked on her coffee. "You what?"

Kate stood and walked to the balcony. "I had an idea I could get some material for a new strip." She glanced over her shoulder and shrugged. "Kinda weird, huh? Somehow at the time it seemed reasonable."

"Reasonable," Heather echoed in a dazed voice. "Reasonable?" She gave an abrupt shout of musical laughter. "I don't know why I'm so surprised." She shook her head, her dark hair bouncing in lively curls. "On the surface you're so sane and practical, but every so often something comes over you and you're convinced that you can manipulate the world around you to suit your own purposes."

Heather sighed and gave her friend a chastising glance, then as though she couldn't help it she grinned. "Well . . . . did you? Get any material, I mean? And more important, did you meet anyone interesting?"

Interesting? Kate thought, smothering a short laugh. *How about fascinating? How about sexy enough to knock your socks off?*

She shook her head at the memory, knowing

she would never speak of the man she had met under the stars. She glanced back at her impatiently waiting friend.

"Oh, yes," Kate said with dry humor. "I met a man who blew in my ear all night and said things in French I'm glad I couldn't understand."

Heather leaned forward, resting her forearms on the table. "That sounds intriguing. Who was he?"

"I don't remember," Kate said, shrugging. "And he wasn't intriguing. Believe me, I've met a lot of human beings in my life and he wasn't among them. When he first attached himself to me, I mistakenly thought he would introduce me to the people whom I had gone there to meet. It didn't take me long to figure out that he wanted to introduce me to things that had nothing to do with society . . . at least not the kind of society I know about." She wiggled her eyebrows expressively.

Heather smiled. "Come on. He can't be the only man you met the whole night. Alexandre Delanore's guest lists for parties are always impressive. You should have met a ton of men."

"I might have met them if I had been able to see them, but unfortunately I had to leave my glasses in my purse." She grinned. "They didn't exactly go with the little gold dress. And besides," she added, "my false eyelashes kept knocking them off."

"You're crazy. Crazy and wonderful," Heather said, then inhaled in happiness. "I'm so glad you're here, Katy," she said exuberantly. "I've missed you."

"Sure you have," Kate said skeptically. "Evan treats you like a princess, you live in a minivilla in the most romantic country in the world and hobnob with the rich and the famous . . . sure you missed me."

"Well, I have," she said. Then she let out a shriek. "Evan! Omigosh, we're supposed to meet him in the Old City for lunch." She jumped to her feet. "If we're going to visit the Oceanographic Museum before then, I've got to get dressed now."

Kate laughed. Even disasters were embraced enthusiastically by her petite friend. Giving a last, lingering glance at the scenery, Kate moved to follow Heather and prepare for the sightseeing and lunch that were planned.

Only cars owned by permanent citizens could enter the city of Monaco, so Heather and Kate took a cab to the Old City, but even with all the rushing they had done they hadn't allowed enough time to see all that the museum contained.

Kate hated rushing through the exhibits, but let her friend set the pace. She was allowed to catch her breath only after they were seated at a table in the center of a small, elegant restaurant.

Kate glanced around the room, then turned her gaze back to Heather. "I don't think I've thanked you yet for asking me to stay with you," she said warmly. "I only hope it isn't putting you out too much . . . because to tell you the truth I was getting sick of hotels."

"Don't be silly. We're so excited about having you. When I got your letter saying you were coming, I literally squealed," Heather said emphatically. "No, I mean it. Our next-door neighbor thought Evan was beating me."

Heather smiled wickedly as though the thought pleased her and Kate wondered again how two people as different as Evan and Heather had fallen in love.

Petite, dark-haired Heather had been scatterbrained all her life—vivacious, good-natured, and outgoing, but still thoroughly scatterbrained. Tall, thin Evan was her exact opposite. He was quiet, introspective, and solid as a rock. When they had first met Heather had described him as being "so stable, he's positively inert." But somehow, against all odds, their marriage had worked beautifully. They were as much in love today as they had been when they married six years ago.

"Where *is* Evan?" Kate asked suddenly, interrupting Heather's enthusing.

"He said he would be a little late." She glanced down at her watch. *"Da-yum."* Heather still had the habit of emphasizing her more earthy expressions by giving them extra syllables. "He'll be here in a couple of minutes and I was going to put on a new face before he came." She stood up in a flustered motion. "You distract him until I get back."

"So Evan gets to see a new face, but a lifelong friend has to make do with the old," Kate said in indignation as her friend turned away.

Heather glanced back over her shoulder and grinned. "If you didn't cut me dead after I gave myself my first permanent, nothing will faze you." She patted her hair and added haughtily, "Evan still thinks I'm naturally beautiful and I don't want to disillusion him."

Kate watched Heather until she disappeared, then, her smile fading, glanced down at her hands. It was strange that she never thought of marrying until she was around Heather and Evan.

But it was always a passing thought, a small ache that was not easily pinpointed. Besides, she thought in a flash of uncomfortable insight, perhaps she was too selfish to be able to make a success of the kind of relationship her friends had.

The kind of love they had involved a commitment Kate felt she was unable to give. Being responsible for another person's happiness was too heavy a load to carry. And depending on someone for one's own happiness was too uncertain a proposition for her practical character to handle.

The stubborn lines of her face softened as she saw Evan walking toward her. Although he wasn't from Plum as she and Heather were, he seemed to represent home . . . or perhaps it was security that he represented, but Kate didn't want to admit to herself that any man could do that.

Whatever emotion he called forth in her, it was enough to make her stand and walk into his thin arms to receive his gentle embrace of greeting.

"Wonderful," she said, laughing in chagrin at the tears in her eyes. "Why am I so glad to see someone as homely as you? You do a Gary Cooper impression without ever opening your mouth."

"You're probably weak from hunger," he said, releasing her, then moving to sit at the table beside her. "I'm sorry I'm late." He glanced around the room. "Where's the addlepated love of my life?"

"She decided you would divorce her if you saw her without lipstick, so she's making repairs." Kate paused thoughtfully. "Why is it that after six years you both still seem like honeymooners?"

He smiled and leaned back in the delicate chair that looked incongruous beneath his lanky frame. "I suppose it's because we still practice being in love. We haven't perfected it yet, so we always have to keep trying." He shrugged his shoulders and looked embarrassed at having revealed so much of himself. "Now tell me about you, Kate. How are you? How's the cartoon business?"

"You had to ask, didn't you?" she said with a

grimace. "I'm thinking seriously of opening a car wash."

"That bad, huh?"

"That bad," she confirmed. "But I don't want to talk about it now. Tell me what's been happening since I saw you last . . . I've already had Heather's version; now I'd like the truth."

He laughed and began to fill her in on how they lived their lives in Monte Carlo. She had to suppress a grin when she realized that he even talked like Gary Cooper.

"So why aren't you married?" Evan asked after a while, his face creased by a wicked grin because he knew how she always avoided that question. "You're twenty-eight years old . . . two years away from the big three-oh. Don't you think it's about time you were settling down?"

She laughed. "The sign of a happily married man. Trying to marry off all his friends." When he continued to stare at her with one expectantly raised eyebrow, she said, "All right, I want to get married, but my astrologer said my sign was in the wrong house . . . or was it that my house was in the wrong sign? Come to think of it, it may have been Jupiter that was in the wrong house. If there are headlines about him breaking and entering, we'll know for sure."

"Cut the bull, Katy. I want to see you as happy as Heather and I are."

She grinned. "Honest, I'd get married in a minute, but the man I'm involved with—I've told you about Conan, haven't I? Well, Conan is into heavy metal and until I can adjust to the idea, I think we'd better just go steady."

"Kate."

The quietly spoken word stopped her and she sighed, staring down at her hands. "I don't think

I could ever be in a relationship like yours and Heather's," she said softly. "I'm just not like you."

"So who said it had to be like ours?"

Damn, he was hardheaded. "Evan, I know you want me to be happy, but married doesn't necessarily equal happy. In fact," she added ruefully, "most of the time it's just the opposite." She paused and glanced away from his probing eyes. "Evan, I've tried," she said in a distracted voice. "I really have. But something always stops me before I take the last step. I rationalize by telling myself that whoever I'm considering couldn't possibly be right or I wouldn't have reservations."

"And you realize that's just an excuse?"

"I suppose so . . . oh, I don't know," she said in exasperation. "If it's that hard for me to consider making a commitment, maybe I'm just not marriage material."

Evan smiled indulgently. "You don't believe that and neither do I. You're a giver. And you always let takers attach themselves to you." He laughed as if to counteract the seriousness of what he was saying. "You've never learned how to lean on another human being. You think it would be a sign of weakness so you hide your emotions behind your tough exterior, but, Katy, someday someone will give to you and you'll have to give that hidden part back in return."

Kate shuddered as though a soothsayer had just predicted her demise. The thought of being in the kind of relationship that Evan wanted for her gave her a funny feeling in her stomach. It frightened her and Kate didn't like being frightened. She looked up to change the subject to something less disturbing, then stopped when she saw Evan's eyes trained on something over her shoulder.

"What have you been doing while I was out of town?" Evan murmured, raising his brows.

"Why do you ask like that?" she said, chuckling. "Like I've been planning to rob the casino or something?"

"No, not a robbery," he said. "But you seem to have attracted the attention of a pretty big fish."

She began to turn in her seat, but before she had barely begun to move, she felt the tingling sensation she had felt only on one other occasion in her life. She tightened her fists on the table and let her gaze travel with unerring accuracy to a table in the corner of the room.

Alex was sitting alone, his gaze trained on her steadily. As their eyes met, he lifted his wineglass in a silent toast, smiling slowly. She was suddenly struck with that same, strange tunnel vision that had affected her the night before. Everything disappeared but his smile.

"He came in behind me and I thought at the time he looked at you oddly."

Evan's voice pulled her back to the present and she glanced away from Alex's dark, compelling eyes and found Evan staring at her with an amused expression on his craggy face.

"But now he's staring a hole in your back," he continued. "Where on earth did you meet Alex Delanore?"

"You know him?" she asked hoarsely.

"I wouldn't say I know him," Evan said ruefully, "but in a place this small you see and hear things. I've seen and heard enough to know he's out of my league . . . and yours, come to think of it. How did you manage to attract the attention of this month's celebrity?"

"I—I met him at a party," she stuttered uncomfortably. "But I barely know him. I can't imagine why he's staring at me," she lied. "What do you know about him?"

Evan leaned back and took a sip of wine. "Let's see. He's new on the scene and everyone's darling. He has a château in Lucerne, one in Belgium, and a villa here. The extent of his wealth is a matter of constant speculation as is his background. He likes women and gambling, spends money like water, and if you want to know what toothpaste he uses, I could probably find out for you by this afternoon."

Kate gave a gasp of surprised laughter. "Whew! Are you trying to tell me that there is a touch of gossip floating around this place?"

"A touch?" he asked, laughing. "It's the leisure occupation of ninety percent of the population." He stared at her curiously for a moment, then leaned forward to place his hand on hers. "What's wrong, Katy?"

Suddenly her hand began to tingle crazily, almost burning with the intensity of the sensation, and she jerked her hand away and rose quickly.

"I—I've just remembered something, Evan. I've got to go." She began to move away as she spoke. "Apologize to Heather for me and tell her I'll see her back at the house." Then, without giving him a chance to speak, she walked briskly out of the restaurant.

Outside on the street, she leaned against a white stone building and took deep breaths until her heart stopped pounding. Then she began to walk slowly, feverish thoughts spinning crazily in her head.

Alex stood and moved across the room after Kate. *One of the benefits of being part of the nobility,* he thought dryly as he walked out of the restaurant. *Nobody chases you when you leave without paying the tab.*

Out in the bright sunlight, he saw her walking slowly away from the building. He smiled in enjoyment of the picture she made as a connoisseur of fine art might smile at the Mona Lisa, an appreciative smile certainly, but perhaps containing a particle of ownership as though this beauty had been created especially for him to enjoy.

Last night she had beckoned his senses and he had been dazzled by her. Today . . . today she beckoned his imagination and he was enchanted.

Her long blond hair was in a roll at the base of her neck, reminding him of a beauty from the nineteen-fifties, and to add to the image, a wide-brimmed white hat framed her face. Her white dress was covered with big navy polka dots and tapered from wide lapels to a small waist cinched by a wide white belt. Her image was all innocence and springtime.

For a moment he hesitated, wondering why he was leaving himself open for another rejection. It wasn't because he thought she had anything to do with Tony's trouble; he was positive she didn't . . . well, almost positive. So why was he bent on harassing a woman who obviously wanted nothing to do with him?

Then one of the sayings that Moustafa was constantly throwing at him popped into his head. *The heart has its reasons that reason knows nothing of.*

He smiled, his chin jutting out in determination, and quickened his step.

Suddenly Kate was not walking alone. She turned her head slightly to the side, but she knew already who it was. Alex was calmly striding along at her side, staring straight ahead. Feeling her heart begin to pick up the wild beat again, she increased her pace, trying to ignore his presence.

"You win."

The softly spoken words startled her as much as if they had been shouted.

"I admit it, Duchess," he continued, his deep voice smooth and calm. "Even though you ran out on me last night, I'm still interested."

She stopped walking and looked him over very carefully. "Should I kneel and kiss your hand or simply alert the local press?" she said, smiling sweetly.

When he merely laughed and glanced at her with warm intimacy, she said, "Look, Count, I'm not a duchess. I'm nobody. I'm simply a struggling cartoonist on vacation who chose your party at random to crash because I needed material. That's all," she said firmly.

"You're a cartoonist?" he asked in surprise. "Which cartoon?"

Why did she feel she could hear relief in his voice? What did he think she did for a living, for heaven's sake? She glanced up at him. "*The Dobsons*. Why?"

"*The Dobsons*," he said in recognition, apparently unconcerned with her question. "I used to read that."

"Used to." Her voice was disgruntled. "Would you like for me to turn around so you can stab me in front too?"

"I'm sorry," he said, grinning an apology. "Did I hit a nerve?"

"I guess I'll have to get used to it," she said moodily, then looked around to find they were walking arm in arm down the street. "Alex," she said, sighing in exasperation, "what is all this about?" She glanced up at him, her face held in sober lines. "I've heard a little about you this morning, and it's not that I'm not flattered, but why are you pursuing me?"

He stopped walking and shoved his hands in his pockets, turning his head to stare up at the sky. She waited silently and after a moment he glanced back at her and shrugged, a twisted smile appearing on his stark features.

"I don't know," he said quietly. "I could say you're the most beautiful woman I've ever seen, but you're not."

"You honey-tongued devil, you," she said, choking on the spurt of surprised laughter.

"I could say you're the most interesting person I've ever met, but I've met Richard Nixon," he said, studying the conflicting emotions in her face.

"And there must be at least . . . two women in the world who are sexier than I am," she said, helping him out.

"At least," he said, beginning to chuckle. "And several who are more successful."

"Well," she said, drawing in a deep breath. "We've eliminated why you're not interested in me, now tell me why you are."

"I don't know," he said, shrugging again. "Maybe it's that weird, warm feeling that takes over every time I get close to you."

"You could get the same thing from a cup of cocoa."

He moved closer to her. "No, I couldn't . . . that's just the point. I've never felt it before. Only with you."

Trouble, she thought, backing warily against the wall behind her. There was sincerity in his tone and that was trouble.

"Look, Alex," she said, her voice faint. "I'm glad I make you feel nice, but I still don't understand why you're following me." She raised her chin belligerently. "For heaven's sake, what do you *want*?"

He placed his hand on the wall above her head. "I want you to get naked," he said as though discussing the weather. "I want—"

She gasped and felt hysterical laughter well up inside her. "Wait—forget I asked," she choked out feverishly. "I don't want to know."

"You shouldn't have asked if you didn't want to know," he said simply, tilting her hat brim with one finger so he could see her face as he continued. "I want to see all of you. I want to feel your skin against mine. I want to take down your hair and feel it falling around me when we make love. I want you to burn with as much need as I feel, as I've felt since last night. I want . . . I want it all, Kathryn."

He moved back a little and smiled. "That's what I want. What I'll settle for is getting to know you better. I don't know about you, but I can always use another friend."

Kate leaned against the wall in stupefaction, then opened her brown eyes wide to stare at him. "You— you ought to be locked up," she said hoarsely. "You follow people around and turn them into stewed carrots." Her accusation gained momentum as her muscles decided at last to stay attached to her bones and her strength returned. "Then you smile and calmly say, 'Be my friend.' "

At her first words, he had begun to smile, then, as a red Jaguar whizzed past, he jerked his head around to watch its progress. Kate frowned when she realized that most of what she had said had been lost on him.

"What is it with you?" she asked. "Is this some kind of Jekyll and Hyde freak-out? Because if it is, the minute you start getting prominent brow ridges and hair on the palms of your hands, I'm cutting out. Do you hear me? *Alex*—"

He turned his gaze back to her, a frustrated expression making his harsh features even more harsh. "Son of a bitch," he muttered in exasperation as he glanced back to the street. Then moving his head to look at her again, he set his jaw stubbornly and said, "Come on," as he took her arm and began to urge her toward the street. Raising a hand, he signaled to a silver-blue Mercedes that was slowly moving toward them, and it seemed to Kate that she remembered the car having passed by them several times before.

When a uniformed chauffeur stepped from the car and moved briskly to open the back door, she pulled away from the hand on her arm. "What in bloody hell do you think you're doing?" she squeaked.

"I'm following that car," he said calmly. Then when he glanced down at her, she saw a sparkle of excitement gleaming in his dark eyes. Turning back to the chauffeur, he said, "You go on home, Bernard."

Kate had opened her mouth to tell him what she thought of eccentric millionaires who tried to abduct innocent cartoonists when suddenly a strange expression crossed her features. Seconds later, without comment, she walked to the car and slid in the passenger side, closing the door firmly.

She didn't even mind that a surprised, but triumphant, laugh erupted from Alex's throat. Because now she knew what she should have known the night before. This was the next act.

Four

Kate sat docile and silent as Alex maneuvered expertly through the twisting streets of Monaco. And she didn't speak when they took Rainier III Boulevard through Fontvieille, the tiny principality's industrial district.

But while they drove, her brow held deep grooves, her eyes narrowed, as she tried to solve the puzzle that nagged at her. She mumbled occasionally, arguing with herself, her index finger held aloft each time she reached a point of importance in her silent debate.

Then as they pulled onto the superhighway that ran from Monaco to Nice and the Mercedes shot forward with a sudden burst of speed, she turned to study the man behind the steering wheel. Panic, bewilderment, and self-flagellation had all been thoroughly explored and discarded by the time she began to speak slowly.

"I'm doing it again, aren't I? For the third

time since I've met you—Lord, was it only yester-day?—I'm following you around like a goose." She tapped the knuckle of her forefinger against her teeth for a moment, then added quizzically under her breath, "Maybe it's because I don't get enough lecithin."

His quick grin didn't anger her. It wasn't his fault that she had gone round the bend. No, she thought, shaking her head, he wasn't responsible for the idea that had hit her so forcefully minutes before, so she couldn't blame him for enjoying the situation.

She shook her head and continued in quiet astonishment. "I'm walking down the street and a man I barely know comes up and says, 'We're going to follow that car,' like something out of a low-budget movie."

She waved her hand back and forth in a help-less gesture. "Do I yell for the police? Do I use what I learned in either of my two judo lessons? Do I even say a polite 'No, thank you. Yesterday was my day for being crazy, so I think I'll be sane today'?" She shook her head emphatically, ignor-ing his laughter. "Uh-uh, not me. Not Kate Call-Me-Irresponsible Sullivan. I step into your car like I've been waiting all my life to go on a joy ride with a fugitive from the banana bin." She gave a laugh that was surprisingly genuine, then leaned back in the smooth leather seat, adding in a lazy non sequitur, "I thought you said you drove a Ford."

"I do, but Bernard drives a Mercedes," he said, glancing across at her, then back to the road ahead. "You're very impulsive, aren't you?"

She shrugged and wiggled her outspread fin-gers in a so-so gesture.

"No, you definitely are," he said. "Do you al-ways regret your impulsive actions?"

She considered the question. "Not usually," she said at last. "I generally decide that if I had taken the safe course, it would have been dull at the very least." She shot him a rueful glance. "But you have to remember my impulses normally concern nothing more drastic than buying a hot pink blouse rather than a demure brown one. It's only in the last two days that my impulses have gotten me in over my head."

"That must mean you're growing." He smiled at her dubious glance. "It stands to reason. Your impulses are expanding in scope, so your mind must be too."

"You really think so?" she asked skeptically, glancing at him from the corner of her eye. "You don't suppose it could be simply that after all these years my brain has finally turned to Malt-o-Meal?" She gave a short laugh. "If I keep going at the rate I'm going, I'll most likely be at Happy Acres next week, weaving place mats out of old pantyhose and molding toothbrush holders out of Play-Doh."

He chuckled and reached over to give her a hearty pat on the back. "You're too tense," he chided amiably. "Loosen up. You made a decision; why not relax and enjoy it?"

Had she made a decision? Kate wondered. She supposed she must have because she was here, but it hadn't seemed to her that she had had a choice—unless life or hibernation was considered a choice. Coming with him, being involved with him, had seemed inevitable at the time. It was only after the deed was done that she began to wonder what strange things were going on in her head.

She wondered suddenly if it were something in Alex that was causing her strange behavior or something within herself. Or perhaps it was the two of them. The things she was beginning to feel, her uncharacteristic actions, may not have been possible until the two of them came together.

Turning slightly in her seat, she began to study his face in curiosity. His smile had faded somewhat as his concentration was once again centered on the examination of the cars in front of them on the highway.

She had forgotten that they were on a mysterious mission. With a sigh she turned her eyes forward to search for the red Jaguar, even though she couldn't help thinking that there were questions she should be asking at this point. Silly little questions like, "What are we doing . . . and why on earth are we doing it?"

But she *wouldn't* ask those questions. Even though she couldn't keep herself from being curious or stop the grumbling protests that were second nature to her, it somehow seemed important that she accept what was happening without waiting for explanations.

After all, would Lois Lane ask Superman for unimportant details when he was zooming away to catch the bad guy? Would the faithful Bullwinkle be anything less than staunch while following the brave Rocky?

Suddenly Kate grinned. Superman? Bullwinkle? It must be an occupational hazard.

"There he is," Alex said at last, suppressed excitement showing through his casual tone. Within seconds they had swung off the highway and were on a small back road, heading roughly north.

"Duchess?"

Kate glanced at him warily when he gave her

a coaxing smile. She definitely didn't trust that smile. "Yes, Count?" she murmured cautiously.

"If you'll open the glove compartment, you'll find a road map," he said, giving her a slightly sheepish look. "Would you look on it and see where we're headed?"

"You mean you don't even know where we are?" she asked, turning to stare at him incredulously.

The feeling that meeting him and becoming involved in his life was somehow fate had been dissolving steadily as they drove; now it disappeared completely. This wasn't her life; it was a missing episode of *The Katzenjammer Kids*.

"I'm from Wisconsin," he said flatly, giving an unconcerned shrug. "If you want to know how to get from Waukesha to Sheboygan, I'm your man. This place could be on Mars and I wouldn't know the difference."

Wisconsin. He had told her the night before he wasn't Belgian and his accent had told her he was American, but it was only now sinking in just how strange that was.

He had told her nothing of his background. How did a man who was as American as football get to be a Belgian count? As far as she knew, titles were always inherited. Evan had told her Alex was new on the Monte Carlo scene. Did that mean that he had only recently become a count, or did it simply mean he was just now getting around to visiting the playground of the rich and the famous?

"Does Wisconsin grow many counts?" she asked, giving him an inquisitive glance. "I mean, is it the state crop or something, like Idaho potatoes?"

When his only response was that brown velvet

chuckle that somehow had the ability to invade her nervous system, she swallowed roughly and gave up her imitation of the loyal Bullwinkle.

"Alex," she said slowly, "I really don't want to pry, but could you tell me why we're chasing after that car? Does he owe you money . . . or are you simply personally offended by red Jaguars?"

"I need to talk to him. A little matter of extortion," he said. His voice was bland and casual, but she could sense he was waiting for her reaction.

"Oh, that explains it," she said, nodding as though she encountered extortion on a daily basis. Leaning forward, she got the map from the glove compartment and spread it out, beginning to examine it closely.

He laughed. "You're adorable, aren't you?"

"I've always thought so," she said modestly, then followed a line on the map with her index finger. "It looks like we're on this thin red line that goes to Digne. You know, Alex, I think I much prefer the big orange double line. It somehow looks more . . . more stable. This one seems to be taking us through a lot of wavy green stuff."

"That wavy green stuff is mountain." His words confirmed the fear she hadn't wanted to voice.

"I think I saw this scene in a movie once," Kate said under her breath as they began to climb a steep, winding road.

"Oh?"

"Yeah, Fred Flintstone and Barney were—" She broke off and caught her breath as he accelerated.

The scenery began to whiz past in a dark green blur. Kate remained cool and calm for at least three seconds, then, as she slumped back in the seat, the wide brim of her hat slid down on her forehead while she squeezed her eyes shut and held on for dear life.

We're going over the edge now, she assured herself, giving a fatalistic nod. *Any minute our path will be vertical instead of horizontal.*

Broken bones were painful. Hadn't she always heard that? Hadn't everyone always told her, "Kate, broken bones are not nice things"? She was very much afraid that any minute she was going to find out firsthand. Come to think of it, forcefully intruding on a glass windshield wouldn't exactly be a maypole dance.

Opening one eye cautiously, she peeked out the side window. Objects she assumed were trees and rocks flew past at a dizzying speed, melting into each other on a blue background in a crazy gray-green, tie-dyed mural.

Dropping her gaze, she stared down at a sheer plunge which seemed to be directly beneath her, as though the tires on her side of the car were supported by nothing more than her desperate grip on the armrest.

If Kate had looked more closely, she would have seen that there were a good three feet between her and the cliff edge, but somehow it didn't seem the time for objective observations and she squeezed her eyes shut once more.

God, can we talk? Kate moaned silently. *I've never asked You for much, have I? You have to understand that I still have things to do.* She drew in a shaky breath. *I have two books overdue at the library and You'll remember I always promised myself that I would run in the Boston marathon . . . just as soon as I got in shape.*

Alex gave Kate a quick glance from the corner of his eye. *She has guts*, he thought with a grin. The speed that was necessary to keep up with

Alvarez obviously scared her silly, but she wasn't going to show it.

Courage and beauty, he thought with delight, *a terrific combination.* It was no wonder he had been intrigued from the first moment he had seen her.

But last night, as he watched her through the window, he had merely thought her attractive . . . and sexy as hell. She had observed the scene around her, completely unimpressed by the people who were so terribly impressed with themselves. That had interested him, but he had been interested by many women only to find later that some flaw in their personality would put him off completely.

It was when he had seen the laughter in Kate's eyes and had recognized unashamed honesty in her reactions to him and the world that he had felt her touch a part of him that ached to be touched. The deepest part, the part that remained lonely even when he was with someone physically.

She had walked into his life and, seemingly without effort, had made him feel more alive than he had felt in years. There was something special about this woman Kate, and he was determined not to let her go until he had discovered what it was that made him feel the way he did.

He chuckled softly when he saw her slide lower in the seat. First, he thought, he would have to find a place that didn't terrify her.

"How're you doing, Katy?" Alex asked, breaking in on her frantic thoughts.

"Fine," she squeaked, the word barely audible. "Fine and dandy." Her last word slid away on a low moan and she resumed her silent conversation with that all-important Someone.

Dying is for Monday mornings in Plum, God,

*not for expensive vacations in France. I promise
. . . I promise I'll never let crazy men pick me up
again if You'll just prevent me from being swept
up by a broom.*

At last Kate knew how the word "bloodcurdling"
originated. She could actually feel the blood flowing through her veins as if it were solid instead of
liquid. Perhaps if she watched, she would be able
to see it moving in lumps beneath her skin. But
she would never know because it would have taken
a crowbar to pry her eyes—

"There he is," Alex said, once again interrupting her wild thoughts.

He sounded calm and sane, but she could
hear the tension underlying his words. And with
murder in her heart, she also recognized excitement. The big oaf was actually enjoying himself.

The idea of throttling him was discarded when
she remembered he was driving, and she opened
her eyes to see the red sports car ahead. Only a
van and a small Saab wagon separated the Jaguar
from the Mercedes. She inhaled in relief as he
reduced their speed and began to maintain a careful distance from the sports car.

Straightening from her slumped position, Kate
picked up the hat that had somehow landed on
the floor and gave it a sorrowful glance. It was
pitifully crushed and bedraggled. Another score
she owed Alex, she thought as she tossed the hat
in the backseat.

"You weren't scared, were you?" How could
he sound concerned and amused at the same time?

"Me?" she scoffed weakly. "Of course not. I
have absolute confidence in your driving."

"I see." He nodded slowly in agreement. "That's
why you ripped off the armrest and wore a hole in
the carpet trying to put on the brake."

She gave an airy wave of her slim fingers. "You know how it is. My mind has confidence in you, but my body's main concern is self-preservation." She lifted an almost steady hand to smooth her tousled blond hair. "It always takes over when I'm that near death."

He laughed, then she caught her breath as the gleam of excitement returned to his eyes and he said, "Hold on, Katy love. He's picking up speed again."

"Ohhh, *day-um*," she wailed, at last seeing the logic in Heather's drawn-out expressions.

Actually, my life wasn't that dull, she thought as she was once again pressed back in the leather seat by the force of their speed. *And anyway, is dull really that bad? I can live with dull. That is, if I live, I can live with dull.*

She cut off the giggle that was rising in her throat. *I will not become hysterical,* she told herself slowly and carefully, but when he passed the ancient Saab on a blind curve, she knew she had lied. Clearing her throat, she tested her vocal chords for the protest whose time had finally come.

"Alex," she said, unable to recognize as her own the thin voice coming from her throat. "Alex, I'm not cut out for this cloak-and-dagger stuff. I'm really not."

"We're going to be friends, aren't we?" He didn't fool her for a minute with his sincere, kind tone. "Friends share experiences."

"Couldn't we share a glass of wine instead?" Then as they burst through a pass and were once again riding on the edge of a cliff, she gulped and added weakly, "On second thought, make that a double vodka."

This time when he laughed she wasn't so

complacent about accepting his amusement, not even when he said bracingly, "You're doing fine."

"Compared to what—cardiac arrest?" she asked dryly, then slid liquidly lower as he swerved slightly to miss a rabbit.

After that she felt not the slightest urge to open her eyes again or even to voice a protest. For what seemed like hours she avoided thinking about the way the car seemed occasionally to slide sideways by reciting the racier bits of Robert Burns poetry that she and Heather had memorized as teenagers.

Kate had gone past racy and was well into bawdy by the time she felt the car slow down. " 'The wildbirds sang, the echoes rang, while Damon's arse beat time, Sir,' " she finished, opening her eyes cautiously.

She glanced first at Alex, unwilling to look out the side window again, and saw that his large frame was shaking with silent laughter.

"I've—" he began in a choked voice. "I've never met anyone who had *all* of Robby Burns memorized."

"Not all. Just the parts that would interest a randy teenager and the one where he plows up a mouse's house." She chanced a peek out the windshield and saw below them a small valley, dotted with houses. "Is that Shangri-La?"

"You know," he said, smiling, "that may have felt like the Himalayas, but, comparatively speaking, they were very small mountains."

"I rarely speak comparatively," she said with acerbity. "So please just tell me straight-out—are we through with that crazy roller-coaster ride and can you find a nice flat way to get me home?"

"Home?"

He said the word reflectively, his voice quiet

and casual. So why did she feel uneasy about that one word?

"Yes, home," she repeated. "My temporary home with my friends in Monte Carlo."

"Actually, Kate—" he began, then his eyes narrowed as he stared down below them into the green valley. "He's stopped. Close your eyes one more time, Katy. I want to see what he's doing."

Perhaps it was his automatic acceptance of her cowardice or perhaps she was getting used to terror, for, whatever the cause, the fast trip down the last incline leading to the small valley didn't even cause her heart to start pumping.

She was quite proud of herself when they passed the empty sports car slowly and pulled over to the side of the road beneath a stand of trees.

"He must be stopping for lunch," Alex said, almost to himself.

"Lunch?" Kate said hopefully. She had missed her lunch. Heavens, that seemed days ago. Glancing down at her watch, she found to her amazement that only two hours had passed since she had left Evan at the restaurant.

"Did you miss lunch too?" Alex asked with a wistful sigh. "I'm starving. And I have a feeling he's at the only tavern for miles around." He glanced back toward the village. "Why don't we go back and see what we can find?"

The tiny village consisted of an inn, an automobile garage with a lean-to-type structure attached to it that reminded Kate of a blacksmith's shop, a beautiful little church made of white stone, and a general store.

And the store was definitely general. It carried everything from freshly baked loaves of French bread and postcards to hammers and lipstick.

While Alex shopped, Kate used the store's phone to put through an overdue call to Heather.

The receiver was picked up on the first ring. "Heather?" Kate said, wondering for the first time just exactly how she would explain to her friend.

"Kate!" came Heather's frantic screech. "Katy Sullivan, where in hell are you? Why did you leave the restaurant like that? Evan said Alex Delanore followed you out. Kate, what on earth is going on?"

"Heather," Kate said, holding back her laughter with difficulty. "I'm fine. Evan was right. Alex followed me out and . . . and invited me to take a ride in the country with him. I just wanted to call and let you know the white slavers didn't get me."

"Alex Delanore," Heather gasped weakly. "How do you know— No, never mind that now; you can explain it all later. Just tell me when you're coming home."

Kate glanced over her shoulder and saw Alex at the counter, paying for his purchases. "I don't know, but don't worry about me; I'm fine. I just never imagined the second act would be quite so exciting."

"The second act? Have you been drinking?" Her voice became suspicious. "Kate, we don't know Alex Delanore very well; are you sure you can trust him?"

Kate didn't answer for a moment. She had known Alex for two days. Did she trust him? Across the room Alex smiled at her and began to walk toward her with his purchases.

"Yes, I do," she said softly, without reservation. "I trust him. I'd better go now, Heather. I'll see you . . . when I see you," she added vaguely, then replaced the receiver and turned to walk out of the store with Alex.

*   *   *

"Okay, I'll accept that," Alex said, taking another bite of cheese. "But if Lillian Gish is the all-time best actress, who's your candidate for the best actor?"

Kate took a sip of the wine they drank from brown pottery mugs and leaned her head back against the leather seat. They had returned to his car to eat their impromptu lunch in order to watch the road for the red Jaguar.

"Best actor, huh? That's a lot tougher. I can be objective about women because I don't fall in love with them, but men are different. The ones I prefer may not be the best actors; they may simply appeal to something in me." She reached into a bag on the seat to secure another handful of grapes. "You would be a better judge of best actor."

"Hmmm," he murmured thoughtfully. "We're talking about pure talent, right?"

She merely nodded in affirmation because her mouth was full of grapes.

"Then I guess I would have to say Lon Chaney."

"Do you really think so? I'll grant you he was a master of what he did, but to me acting is the ability to change characters without the makeup and all the external devices he used," she explained as she stole a piece of his cheese and took a reflective bite. "Becoming the character on the inside rather than on the outside."

He paused in tearing off another piece of bread. "Maybe," he conceded at last. "If that's so, then I guess my vote would have to go to Theodore Roosevelt."

"Disqualified," she said, laughing and choking on her wine at the same time. "Politicians aren't allowed." She paused. "Can't you just see awards handed out every year for the politician who has fooled the most people into thinking he knew what he was doing?"

"Are we going to talk politics?" he asked warily as he cleared away the remains of their meal and placed the bag in the backseat.

She tapped the mug against her chin, considering the question. "No," she said at last. "We're not. The sun's shining, I'm in France, and I'm full of good food. If there ever was a day for not discussing politics, this is one."

"Good," he said with a satisfied sigh as he leaned back in the seat. "Okay, tell me Elvis's all-time best record."

She considered the question for a moment, then finished her wine and placed the cup in the backseat. "It's a toss-up," she said at last. "Between 'That's All Right, Mama' and 'I Want You, I Need You, I love You.' "

"You're not even considering 'Jailhouse Rock'?" he said in amazement.

"Uh-uh," she said, shaking her head emphatically. "Maybe 'Teddy Bear,' but not 'Jailhouse Rock.' "

"Philistine," he said in disgust. "You obviously have a tin ear."

She laughed at his offended expression, then leaned back in the leather seat, drinking in the fresh country air.

He looked around them at the countryside. "Doesn't the air feel different here, Kate?" he said, echoing her thoughts. "It's not just that the people speak a different language and the houses are different. There's a different feel to France than there is to the United States . . . at least to my part of the United States."

"Yes, it's different," Kate said. "But I've felt it before. In Texas. We don't get much in the way of a change in seasons so when we do it's something that sticks in your memory. The few days of spring and fall that we have always make me remember things that have happened in other springs, other falls." She smiled in reminiscence. "This reminds me of the first time I fell in love."

"Painful or happy?" he asked, giving her an understanding glance.

"Definitely happy. He had me totally captivated while it lasted, then let me down easy when it was over."

"I can't imagine you being captivated," he said, and there was something close to envy in his expression. "How did this paragon of virtue manage it?"

"He had blond curly hair, clear blue eyes, and lots of money for a start," she said, curling her legs up beside her and resting her chin on her hand. "But I think maybe the thing that really made me fall head over heels for Billy Wayne Turner was his ability to make the most remarkable noises simply by putting his hand under his arm."

"He sounds like pretty tough competition," he said, chuckling. "I think I probably fell in love for the first time in grade school too."

"Grade school?" she said, raising an arched brow. "It was last year."

She loved to see him laugh. He did it with such enjoyment and the rich sound always spread through her blood like brandy, warming her completely. For a moment she felt that if she were suddenly given one wish it would be to spend the rest of her life listening to his laughter.

She shook the thought away, wondering in astonishment what had gotten into her. A sentimental wish like that was just not like her.

"Kate?" He shifted his position slightly so that

he was much closer than before, lifting a hand to smooth a stray curl back from her forehead. "We've eaten and we've talked and it still looks like we have some extra time on our hands." His fingers drifted down to rest on her shoulder so that his arm was around her. He stared down at her with a hopeful expression. "You wanna neck?"

She gave a choking gasp of laughter. "*You wanna neck?* Geez, how romantic can you get?"

"I'm not romantic," he said with an unselfconscious shrug. "I thought you had figured that out by now. That doesn't mean I'm not exciting and terrifically sexy. So how about it?"

She almost choked on her indrawn breath. He thought he was teasing about being exciting and sexy, but actually he had hit it right on the nose. She had been trying with difficulty all afternoon to keep her thoughts away from the way she had felt last night.

"No," she said, giving a shaky laugh at the lie. "I don't. I would really like for you to tell me a little more about what's going on." She glanced up at him to study his strong face carefully. "You haven't given me an awful lot of information up to now."

His dark eyes met hers as she spoke and after a moment of silent communication, he shrugged. "I may be wrong," he said softly, "but I got the idea that you had reasons of your own for coming with me. Reasons that had nothing to do with why I'm chasing that man."

How could he know that? How could he know that Kate had viewed their meeting and the subsequent events as a kind of challenge that life was throwing at her, a challenge she had to meet or be condemned to accept her ordinary existence as unworthy?

She glanced away from him uneasily and said,

"Okay, I'll accept that, but now I'd really like to know more about what's happening."

"It's a long story. One that starts a lot of years ago." His eyes took on a faraway look. "What's important is that an old friend of mine is being blackmailed."

A chilled shiver ran up her spine. She had taken everything so lightly until now, but this was not something she could shrug off. She wanted to ask more—who and why—but blackmail indicated a need for secrecy. She couldn't ask him to give away secrets that weren't his to give. "By the man in the Jaguar?" she asked quietly.

He was silent for a moment. "I don't think so. Don't ask me why. He's the man who is making the demands, but somehow it just doesn't jell." He shrugged. "So I'm following him to try and get to the bottom of the thing. I want to know who's behind it and why. I also need to recover some things that are potentially harmful to my friend's well-being."

"Do you know the man in the car?"

"I've met him," he said, his voice grim. "Our man is one René Alvarez, born in Paris of Spanish parents. He's been a hanger-on for most of his life and—as far as I can tell—will do anything for money." He swirled the wine in his cup, concentrating on the ruby liquid, then gave a rough sound of frustration. "In the last few months I've been to enough parties to last me a lifetime. I've cultivated Alvarez and his friends, trying to make some sense out of the whole thing. I've purposely acquired a . . . a tainted reputation so that he would feel free to brag about what he's doing."

Kate's eyes widened in surprise. So he knew what people were saying about him. And he didn't sound as though he enjoyed the reputation he had gained.

"And did he?" she asked, without comment.

He laughed harshly before tipping back his head to finish the last of the wine in his mug. "He's bragged about using and selling several illegal drugs," he said without looking at her. "He's bragged about being the go-between in an art swindle and about other activities that you wouldn't want to hear about, but so far, not one word about Tony."

"Your friend?"

He nodded. "I can't figure out the connection," he said emphatically, rubbing the back of his neck with his free hand. "And the more he talks the more I believe he's only a hired messenger."

She gave him an inquisitive glance. "You mean someone picked him up at the local 'Hoods "R" Us'?"

"Something like that." He chuckled. "No, if this whole blackmail scheme were his idea, he'd have asked for money right away and that would have been the end of it . . . until he wanted more. But there have been no demands for money. Someone wants Tony to suffer."

She glanced down at her hands for a moment, mentally putting a lid on her curiosity as she recognized the sincerity, the urgency in his voice. "What demands have there been . . . if not for money?" she asked.

"In the beginning, Tony merely received letters that let him know that someone was in possession of certain . . . facts concerning his past." Alex's features were grim as he spoke. "Then they started to become more threatening." He paused. "Tony has been offered a wonderful opportunity, an opportunity that could change his whole life.

Whoever wrote the letters wants him to give up that opportunity . . . or they will make certain things from his past public."

She examined his face in detail, the worried lines around his eyes, the sternly held lips. "This is really important to you, isn't it?" she asked finally.

"Tony's important to me," he said quietly. "It's not often that you get to pay back a debt the size of the one I owe Tony. I won't let the chance go by. I'll fix this for him because I owe him and because I love him."

She had never heard a man confess his love for another man. But there was no hesitation in Alex's voice, no embarrassment. In her eyes he grew another three feet, and there in a car parked outside an unknown village in France, Kate thought for a moment she had glimpsed the beginning of the third and most important act of her life.

As though he read the change in her eyes, Alex caught his breath and began to lean slowly closer. "This time I won't ask," he said softly, then bent the final few inches to press his lips against hers.

And this time she wouldn't have said no, she thought as she felt the warmth of his full lips on hers. She closed her eyes and waited for the powerful sensations that were caused only by Alex to return to her.

But it took only a few seconds for her to realize that it wasn't at all like it had been the night before. Then she had been confused, even frightened, by the new feelings he aroused. Now, as the vibrating warmth raced through her limbs, she felt as though his touch and the accompanying pleasure were things she had been waiting for forever.

Although her feelings were even more powerful than they had been the night before, she no longer felt threatened by them. It was as though her body had finally accepted the strange sensations as a part of her.

Her lips parted naturally beneath his and the kiss deepened by mutual consent. Groaning, he slid his seat back and pulled her into his lap. "I was wrong," he whispered, staring into her eyes. "Kathryn is not for making love. Kathryn is too cold for someone as warm and receptive as you are. You're Katy . . . my Katy love."

He moved his head the fraction of an inch it took to cover her lips and she received him hungrily as though he had been away for years instead of seconds. His fingers were spread wide on her rib cage, resting just below her breast, and she felt every centimeter of the flesh there as though his touch magnified ordinary sensation.

He pressed her down against him, flexing his thighs slightly at the same time, and the delicious magnification spread to other aching places. A pulsing need grew within her, urging her to get closer and even closer.

He pulled back, just a breath away, and touched her lips with his tongue, then leaned the side of his head against hers, his breathing unsteady.

She stared straight ahead and after a moment whispered a soft, breathless "Wow."

Alex made a rough noise that could have been a laugh. He sounded breathless too. "I was thinking something more along the lines of *hot damn*!"

With a hand on her neck he turned her head back toward him. When she moved a flash of red caught her peripheral vision. As his lips grazed hers, she murmured, "Aren't we supposed to be watching for the Jaguar?"

"Hmmm?" he said against her lips.

"The red sports car. The . . . um . . . the—" She forgot what she had intended to say as he deepened the kiss.

"The sports car?" He dipped his head to her neck, then sat up straight. "The Jaguar! Hell and damnation," he muttered, running a hand through his hair and down his neck. "He could at least have stayed for dessert."

As he touched her swollen lower lip with one rough finger, his eyes held deep regret. "I guess it's time to move on, Katy love."

It took a while for Kate to regain her equilibrium. He left her dazed and she felt she should be analyzing the strange things that were happening to her mind and her body.

But she couldn't. All she could think about was how beautiful the day was and how wonderful she felt.

Alex had begun to whistle as soon as they were on the road again, but she had been too absorbed to listen. Now she smiled, recognizing the song.

A fine romance.

Five

Shifting his position slightly, Alex flexed his stiff shoulder muscles. The sun was hanging low in the west as he glanced at the digital clock on the console, then across at the woman sleeping beside him.

Kate was curled up in the reclined leather seat, her hands forming a pillow under her cheek. She had had a rough day and most likely a confusing one.

Sighing gustily, he told himself he probably shouldn't have dragged her into this. It wasn't her affair and if nothing else it could get a little sticky. But to be fair to himself, he hadn't realized Alvarez would be leaving the area around Monaco. If he had known . . .

He smiled. If he had known he probably would have done the same thing. On the street back there in the Old City, it had seemed vitally important that he keep her with him, as though a voice inside his brain were telling him that it was his only chance with Kate.

He wished suddenly that he could have met her when he wasn't involved with this blackmail business. But then if he hadn't been involved in it, would he have gotten to know her so quickly? Wouldn't they have had to go through the routine of dating and slowly learning to know each other before they even reached the point they were at now?

A rueful smile twisted his lips. If it took a high-speed chase to get close to her, then he was glad it had happened just the way it did. When they returned to Monte Carlo—

Alex broke off his thoughts with a smothered exclamation. He had forgotten all about Paul. He should have called him when they stopped for lunch to let him know what was happening. Yes, he should have called, but his thoughts had been completely taken over by Kate.

He grinned in anticipation when he thought of her temper and the way she would react when she woke up and found they couldn't make it back to Monte Carlo tonight.

Reaching over, he gently touched her shoulder. "Kate. Katy love, wake up."

She moved her head until her cheek rested on his hand, then rubbed against it like a contented cat. It seemed that Kate could be tamed, but only in her sleep.

Chuckling, he said, "Kate, we've already passed Lyon; is that all right?"

She stirred slightly, her lips curving in a lazy smile. It was a smile that took his breath away. "Lyon?" she murmured sleepily. "Lyon's nice."

He realized she hadn't come fully awake, but at least he had tried. Lifting his hand, he brushed back a golden curl from her temple, then reluctantly returned his full attention to the highway and the car ahead.

Some time later Kate felt warmth on her lips, then her ear. "What are you doin'?" she murmured.

"I'm kissing you."

That sounded reasonable. "Why're ya doin' that?" she asked drowsily, not really caring why, but feeling obligated to ask anyway.

" 'Cause all of a sudden, I had a cravin' flung upon me," he drawled and kissed her again.

"Are you making fun of the way I talk?" she said. Her Texas accent lost some of its strength as she came fully awake.

"Who, me?" he asked guilelessly.

She pulled herself upright. "Where are we?" Moving stiffly at first, she stretched her cramped muscles. She glanced out the side window at the growing darkness, then her eyes narrowed as she caught sight of the small structure beside the car. "Is that a barn?" she asked slowly. "It *is* a barn." She swung around to face him, her eyes wary. "Alex, why are we parked beside a barn?"

"Because he stopped for the night," Alex said, opening the car door. "Alvarez stopped at the inn in town and took a small suitcase out of the car."

"Yes? Go on," she prompted expectantly. "That still doesn't explain why *we're* parked beside a barn."

"It was the only inn in town—"

He had begun to step out of the car, but she stopped him with a hand on his arm. "And?"

"And if we stayed there for the night he would see us," he said, smiling as though he had said something wonderfully reasonable.

"If we stayed the night—" She broke off, too stunned to continue.

"So I found this place." He sounded extremely pleased with himself as he continued enthusiastically. "I checked at the house and the people are not home. I don't think they'd mind if we used their barn just for tonight. There are no animals in it for us to bother."

Kate stared in amazement. "You're honestly suggesting that we spend the night in that—that cow shed?" she sputtered. She closed her eyes and inhaled deeply, then keeping her voice calm, said, "Alex, dear, call me a cab."

"There are no cabs," he said, not doing a very good job of hiding his amusement. "Probably not very many telephones from the looks of the place."

"Then you'll simply have to take me home," Kate stated firmly, leaning back in the seat to cross her arms in determination.

"It's too far to drive tonight." His midnight eyes were sparkling, but he kept his voice low and soothing. "Do you really want to travel those roads in the dark?"

She turned her head toward him sharply. "Listen carefully—I refuse to spend the night in a place even cows won't sleep in," she said stubbornly. "Do you hear? I refuse."

And Kate was still refusing five minutes later as she watched him bunch up hay on the floor of the small barn.

"Adventure," she muttered under her breath. "I wanted adventure. This is act two, Kate. Fate sent him, Kate," she continued, mimicking her own thoughts. "Well, I certainly got adventure. I'm about to sleep on a pile of moldy hay with a man I've known less than twenty-four hours." Then more loudly, "What kind of bugs do you suppose live in hay?"

He laughed over his shoulder as he went

through the double doors on his way back to the car. A couple of minutes later he returned, still chuckling as he carried in a plaid wool blanket and the bag that contained the remainder of the food he had bought earlier.

While she watched in obstinate silence he spread the bright red blanket over the hay, then removed the meat pies and what was left of the wine. Then he turned to take a kerosene lantern from a hook by the door and raised it for her inspection with an implied "Ta-*dah.*"

She humphed and shifted her stance, folding her arms once more across her middle. She felt silly standing in the middle of an empty barn while he did all the work, but he had to understand that she wouldn't keep on following his every lead. It had to stop somewhere.

After lighting the lamp, he stood and made a sweeping gesture of invitation toward the lumpy picnic spread, his smile gleaming in the dim light.

He looked so pleased with himself that Kate found her resolve quickly crumbling. *Next time*, she thought. Next time she would be firmer. And with that wonderful bit of equivocating, she shrugged and sat down.

She studied him intently for a while, then said, "You know, I think I've finally figured out why you like me."

"Oh?" He ran his eyes over her body with an exaggerated leer. "Little slow on the uptake, aren't you?"

"No," she said, shaking her head. "I'm serious." She picked up a meat pie. "It's because I'm a cheap date. If you were with one of those frou-frou women at your party, she would have expected caviar and champagne and a room at the

Ritz. But good ole Katy Sullivan from Plum, Texas, gets cold meat pies and a pile of hay."

He chuckled. "Champagne and a room at the Ritz, huh? I'll keep that in mind for our second date." When she choked on her pie, he grinned, then said, "Plum," as though he were savoring the word. "I like that. Is it in the middle of a plum orchard or something?"

"As far as I know there isn't a plum tree within fifty miles of Plum. A lot of prickly pear cactus and mesquite trees, but no plums." She paused. "I guess Plum just sounds better than Prickly Pear, Texas."

He poured two mugs of wine and handed one to her. "So you create your cartoon world in Plum, Texas?"

"Actually I don't." She took another bite of the beef-and-mushroom-filled pastry and found it surprisingly good. "I have a place in Dallas and only get to Plum on the occasional weekend." She paused reflectively. "My hometown somehow puts things back into perspective. When I get caught up in the mad rush for success in Dallas and begin to think unimportant things are important, I simply go back to Plum for a while. The people in Plum still treat me like little Katy Sullivan, the girl next door. There are no imagined power struggles there, only very real struggles against the sun and the wind and the rain." She shrugged. "It keeps me whole."

She sent him a slow, appraising glance. "How about you? Do you go back to Wisconsin occasionally to find out who the real Alex Delanore is?"

He shook his head. "It's different with me. I'm only here because of Tony."

"You became a count just to help out your friend?"

"I acquired the title and estate three years ago, but I've actively used my inheritance only in the last six months. That's when Paul and I came to Europe."

"Paul?"

"Paul works for me . . . and he's a personal friend. He came with me to help. You'll like him." He grinned. "I'm afraid neither of us is cut out for this kind of life, but I knew if I were going to get any information I would have to be right here where it was happening." He leaned back to rest on one elbow. "In Madison, I'm just plain Al Delanore. But I know what you mean about keeping you whole. After a month or two of living the good life I began to wonder if I had dreamed my life in Madison . . . or if this was the dream. It's hard to know what's real and that worries me. I never had that problem when I was running my construction company."

Construction. She stared at him in the dim light and a picture began to form—Alex, bare to the waist, tight faded jeans, sweat glistening on the muscles of his tanned body, a hard hat covering his dark hair.

Holy cow, she exclaimed silently, sucking in a stunned breath as the vision started her blood percolating. She cleared her throat roughly and asked, "Do you—do you sit in an office or go out with the men?"

He shook his head, sitting up to rest his forearms on his knees. "I can't stay in the office for long." He tapped his head. "The brain gets dull. Sooner or later, I have to get out where the action is."

She picked up a handful of hay and fanned her face furiously, ignoring his speculative glance. "I'd—I'd like to see you working someday." She looked up and stared at shadows cast on his face. "You know, the first time I saw you I thought you looked like an American Indian. The resemblance is not as strong in the daylight, but now, with the shadows highlighting your cheekbones, you could almost be a Comanche warrior."

He laughed. "There is American Indian blood on my mother's side, but I'm afraid it's Choctaw . . . farmers, not warriors," he added apologetically.

Again a vivid image began to invade her thoughts—Alex, bronzed and bare, wearing a loincloth, his dark hair tied back with a leather thong as he sat astride a sleek horse, carrying a bow and . . . No, not a warrior, she corrected. It didn't matter. He'd look sexy even hoeing corn.

Stop it, she told herself sternly, giving her head a sharp shake. Imagery like that could only lead to trouble, especially since she was about to spend the night with the object of that imagery.

She made impersonal small talk through the rest of their meal, carefully overlooking the gleam in his dark eyes. When he took the remains of their food to the car to keep from tempting any animals that might be about, she stared after him for a moment, then sighed and took off her glasses, putting them in her purse. Her mind was definitely not on her hair as she let it down to begin the familiar nightly ritual.

"Damn, damn, damn," she muttered as the comb snagged again and refused to budge. The tangles she had acquired on her adventure were vicious.

Alex stepped back into the dimly lit barn, then stopped abruptly when he saw Kate kneeling on the blanket, her long hair freed at last.

Lorelei, he thought, sucking in a stunned breath.

He had never seen anything like it. It gleamed like molten gold in the flickering light, flowing over her shoulder to her waist. He suddenly felt as though he had been kicked in the stomach.

When she turned to give him an inquiring glance, he squatted beside her and said gruffly, "Here, let me," taking the comb from her hand.

As he combed, he ran his other hand over the silken mass, surreptitiously picking up a handful to bring it to his cheek. When she shifted her position slightly, he dropped it hastily and cleared his throat.

"I think I've nearly got the tangles licked," he said hoarsely.

She laughed softly. "I don't know why I keep it this way. It's not that I'm especially fond of long hair. I think it's simply to avoid going to a hairdresser. I hate just sitting there for hours when I could be doing something. I'll probably have it cut as soon as I get back home."

"No!" he said quickly, then more calmly, "I don't think you should. Long hair suits you."

She turned slightly, giving him a strange look, and Alex could have kicked himself for his spontaneous reaction. It was only hair, for Pete's sake. Why was it causing him to breathe unsteadily? And why was he having to make such an effort to keep from burying his face in it?

But it wasn't only hair. It was Kate's hair. And there was something incredibly intimate about seeing it down. Perhaps it was because he knew somehow that not many people had seen her like this.

Steeling himself against thoughts that were even more intimate, he got on with the job of smoothing away the tangles.

For a few seconds after he had taken the comb

from her, Kate was grateful for Alex's help. Now she was beginning to realize what an erotic thing having one's hair combed was.

The tingles he produced so easily in her played on her flesh and her senses. Gooseflesh stood out on the nape of her neck at his touch. She had read of proper Victorian ladies swooning when overtaken by strong emotions, but she never thought she would come so close to it herself.

At last, she heard him exhale roughly, then he said, "I think that's got it. We'd better get some sleep now."

Her heart was pounding visibly in her breast as she hastily braided her hair. Afterward she glanced down at her rumpled dress. It wasn't exactly made for sleeping, but she wasn't about to take it off.

Alex didn't speak as he extinguished the light, and she shivered when darkness flooded the barn. *Ghoulies and ghosties and long-legged beasties*, she thought, stifling a semihysterical giggle. Then as her eyes began to adjust to the dark, she felt Alex lie down beside her and "things that go bump in the night" were forgotten.

She held herself stiff for as long as she could, then began to fidget as she felt the lumps of hay poking into her side. She jumped skittishly when he began to punch the blanket beside him. Then he pulled her over until she rested in the indention he had made.

"Are you comfortable now?"

She snorted indelicately. "Sure I am. Didn't I tell you the dream that sustained me into adulthood was spending the night in a place a good wind would blow away?"

"Here, relax against me." He lifted her head,

then shifted and cradled it on his shoulder. "Now, isn't that better?"

She started to answer, but stopped suddenly, holding her breath. She remained silent for a moment, then whispered, "Alex, is—" She stopped to clear her throat. "Is your hand on my breast?"

"What?" He glanced down to where his large hand covered her left breast. "Why, so it is," he said in surprise, then looked back at her and said solemnly, "My hand is definitely on your breast."

She swallowed nervously. "Are you going to take it away?"

His hand tightened a fraction. "Not unless the barn catches on fire," he said gruffly.

When he lowered his head, Kate knew he was going to kiss her. And if he did, it wouldn't stop at a kiss. The tension between them had been building all day, and since he had combed her hair, you could have cut it with a knife.

"Alex," she whispered when his lips were only an inch away. "No."

"No?" He held himself perfectly still, his eyes narrowing as he peered through the darkness to study her features.

She could feel the tautness in him and it caused an ache she couldn't identify. Perhaps she shouldn't have been so abrupt. She wanted to explain, but how could she explain something she didn't fully understand herself?

Suddenly he pulled his arm from beneath her to prop himself up on one elbow. "I see," he said, nodding. "No lips . . . so how about ears?" He swooped down to nip her earlobe. "Or cheeks . . . or a nose . . . or maybe a chin?"

Each time, he suited the action to the word, kissing her faster and faster as she began to laugh and dodge his lips. She knew he was trying to clear the air and she silently thanked him.

"How about a temple? A well-turned temple drives me wild," he murmured against her skin.

"Stop it, you idiot." She laughed.

He lay back, resting his head on his forearm. "On one condition."

"And that is?" she asked warily.

"Let me have half a lip and I'll stop."

"Alex—" she began.

"I know, I know." He sighed roughly and pulled her back to her former position against his shoulder. "You're thinking it's not supposed to happen this fast." He cupped her chin with his right hand. "But, Katy, don't you see? We're lucky. Most people have to spend months, even years, getting to know each other as well as we have in just two days." He stroked her cheek with his rough fingers. "I promise not to push you if you'll promise not to worry about rules and what's 'normal.' "

For a moment she couldn't speak. Did all that really make sense or was it just that she wanted to believe what he was saying?

"Okay," she said at last. "Half a lip."

He laughed, knowing that her okay meant more than a kiss. He cupped her neck and pulled her closer, brushing his lips across the corner of her mouth. Then he exhaled slowly and whispered, "I'm giving serious thought to becoming a monk, Duchess."

"A monk?"

"Yeah," he murmured wryly. "I think I'm beginning to get the celibacy bit down pat."

She laughed softly, snuggling against him as he wrapped his suede jacket around them both.

Six

When Kate awoke Alex was no longer beside her. There was still a chill in the air, but rays of sunshine fell through cracks in the barn door in shafts of platinum-gold.

Wrapping his suede jacket more closely around her, she huddled and thought of the way they had slept with their arms around each other through the night.

Because Kate was a restless sleeper, she had always assumed she wouldn't be able to adjust to sleeping with a man. But with Alex, there had been no fighting for space, no cramped muscles. They had fit together perfectly, their limbs entwined. She realized with surprise how soundly she had slept, as though she had been sleeping with him for years.

Yawning lazily, she wondered where he was now and what he was doing. She felt a little strange, a little empty, then realized it was the first time she had been completely alone since he had followed her from the restaurant the day before.

Who was this Wisconsin count who affected her so strongly? He had told her almost nothing about his past and very little about why they were here. How did she know the little he had told her was true? She had only his word that the unknown man in the Jaguar was an accessory to blackmail.

But before her mind could even get started on that train of thought, she stopped herself with a frown. *No, Kate. It won't work,* she admitted silently. She couldn't even call up the smallest doubt about Alex's sincerity. It had been too strong in his face and in his voice when he had told her about his friend's problem.

It was truth time, she decided in resignation. His reasons for chasing across the French countryside after an unknown man were not important. What was important was why she had chosen to come with him.

Was it really a yearning for adventure or even a belief that fate had brought them together to test her? Or could it be nothing more complicated than the fact that she was attracted to him and wanted to be with him?

She realized ruefully that the last possibility had the ring of truth, but where did that get her? She was attracted to him and he obviously felt the same about her, but she had been attracted to men before, although never like this. Why was this time different? And where was it all leading?

Suddenly she looked up and found Alex kneeling beside her. Quickly she drew a curtain on the thoughts spinning around in her mind and smiled her greeting.

"I was wrong," he said quietly. "Your eyes aren't brown. They're caramel." His voice held amazement, as though he had discovered something miraculous.

Kate lowered her eyes, wishing she had had more time to think about him. This was no ordinary attraction. His tone and the look in his eyes as well as his words brought a flood of warmth to her body. It took a major effort on her part to keep from reaching out to him.

"Good morning," she said as she pulled herself upright, her voice sounding uncharacteristically reserved.

"Good morning." He chuckled. "While you were sleeping I've been busy." He placed a wrapped and tied package in her lap. "I thought you might appreciate a change of clothes. It's only jeans, T-shirt, and sneakers, but at least they won't look like you slept in them."

Kate felt her reserve slip away at his easygoing tone. "Are you suggesting that I'm rumpled?" she asked, glancing at him from the corner of her eye as she tore off the brown paper wrapping.

"On you, rumpled looks stunning," he said gallantly, pulling something from under the stack of clothing.

"A toothbrush!" she exclaimed, cradling the blue brush. "You're an angel. I can't get started until I brush my teeth." She paused and glanced quickly around the small barn, seeing it for the first time in daylight. "Alex . . . um . . . where's the powder room in this hotel?"

"I was afraid you were going to ask that," he said ruefully. "I'm afraid the powder room consists of an outhouse and a pump beside the trough in the yard."

"A pump?" she echoed in astonishment. "I've

never seen a real pump. Are you sure it works? I didn't think anyone still used them."

He nodded, smiling at her pleasure. "It works. It's probably left over from days gone by. I imagine they have running water in—"

"Wait—wait a second," she said, her eyes narrowing. "Did you say outhouse . . . as in half-moon-on-the-door, two-holer, drafts-on-the-cheeks outdoor latrine? That kind of outhouse?"

He nodded, trying to keep his face straight. "I'm afraid so. It's either that or wait until we get to a gas station."

"Some choice," she muttered, then shrugged in resignation. "Never let it be said that Kate Sullivan lacked the pioneer spirit that made America what it is today . . . a place with nice, shiny *indoor* bathrooms."

Ignoring his laughter, she gathered her new clothes together, then stood up, enthusiasm building at the thought of a new day despite the limited facilities. She had felt excitement stirring as soon as she found Alex kneeling beside her. It was like an electric aura that surrounded him, touching her when he was near, but disappearing when he did.

She spent as little time as possible in the small outhouse; quaint was one way she could have described it, however it was not the word that kept popping into her mind. After quickly changing into the things he had bought her—they were just a tiny bit snug—she joined Alex in the yard.

While he worked the handle up and down, she brushed her teeth and washed her face in the water from the ancient pump. It was icy cold, but the novelty of having it pumped right out of the ground kept her mind off her frozen face.

Afterward she sat on a small milking stool and, while she was serenaded by hundreds of birds, she combed and rebraided her hair.

Sitting on a stump, Alex watched Kate work with her hair and suddenly wished they didn't have to leave. He knew it was crazy, but he wouldn't mind sleeping on hay or washing under an ancient pump in the open air if he just could linger a while longer with her.

Something had happened to him as he had held her in his arms the night before. Something wonderful and new and exciting. He found himself dreaming of holding her ten years in the future, twenty years in the future.

He had sat for quite a while that morning watching her as she slept. He was wondering how she would look lying in his bed back in Wisconsin but knowing all the while that she would never look lovelier than she did lying on a pile of hay.

The feeling was strange for Alex. He had desired women before. And he had liked women before. There had even been women that he had both liked and desired, but he had never thought of growing old with any of them. He wanted to grow old with Kate. He wanted to be there when she got her first gray hair. He wanted to watch her play with their children and grandchildren.

The thought of making children with Kate brought an indescribable, fluttering ache to his heart and he felt his stomach muscles tighten as though he were held in the grip of an iron fist.

Breathing deeply, Alex forced his expression to remain normal. He couldn't rush her now. It was too important and he had done too much pushing already. She had to be as sure of him as he was of her.

They ate freshly baked croissants in the open

air, sighing over them as though they were ambrosia and laughing at anything that popped into their heads. It was a morning out of a storybook, a morning to store away in memory and pull out on cold days in the future.

After breakfast, Alex placed a handful of francs under a clay pot sitting on the porch and they left. Back on the road, he positioned the Mercedes behind a deserted shed so that they could watch for Alvarez.

They had waited less than thirty minutes when the Jaguar passed them, and Alex pulled out of their hiding place, following it to the superhighway that ran all the way to Paris.

The highway was much more heavily traveled than the small road they had begun on, but it had the advantage of letting them stay close to the Jaguar without being detected. They passed the time delving into each other's minds and Kate thoughtfully absorbed the memories of Alex's childhood in Wisconsin.

It certainly didn't sound like the background of a count, she realized. His experiences more closely matched those of Tom Sawyer, in fact a normal American childhood. An only child, he seemed to have fond memories of both his parents and she could find nothing in what he told her that suggested anything unusual in his upbringing.

The miles flew by as they talked. Just after one, Alvarez abandoned the highway for a small country road.

"This may be it," Alex said as he dropped back to keep from being seen on the almost deserted road.

"May be what?" Kate asked in confusion, sensing a new tension in him.

"He may be meeting his contact somewhere around here."

Alex sounded as though that were something to be desired, but Kate wondered if she really wanted to be around when the blackmailer was unmasked. The person whom Kate had mentally designated Mr. Big was not someone she was looking forward to meeting.

When the sports car pulled up before a large, slightly garish restaurant, Alex passed it and parked the Mercedes a short distance down the street.

Opening the door, he stepped out, then dipped his head to say, "I'm going in to see what he's doing."

Every gangster movie Kate had ever seen came back to haunt her as she sat in the car waiting for Alex, terrible visions of massacres and assassinations and cement overcoats. Until that moment she hadn't even considered the possibility that what he was doing might be dangerous. She suddenly wanted to run after him and . . . and . . .

Just exactly what would I do? she thought in disgust. Protect him from the bad guys? Ask him to forget about helping his friend?

She shook her head. There was nothing she could do except wait and trust him. He was an intelligent man, a strong man, and she would trust him with her life. Now she would simply have to learn to trust him with his own.

As she rubbed her fingers across her brow in thought, something vague began to nip at the edges of her mind. It concerned Alex and the way he was taking over her every thought. But before she could grasp it, he was back.

He slid behind the wheel and shrugged at her

expectant look. "He's ordering lunch . . . alone," he said, his voice showing his disappointment.

"Alex," she began hesitantly. "Couldn't he simply be on his way to see his parents or a girlfriend?"

"I've considered that possibility," he admitted slowly. "Not that I think he would be visiting his parents; he's not the sentimental type. But he could be on business that has nothing to do with Tony." He shrugged. "I just couldn't take the chance. For weeks now Paul has been following him around in Monte Carlo during the days, while I wined and dined the bastard at night. And neither of us has come up with one solid fact. He doesn't seem to have met secretly with anyone." He tightened his fingers on the steering wheel. "It has to be now or we're down to beating the truth out of him."

She reached over to cover one of his large hands with hers and gave it a reassuring squeeze. "It'll work out. You'll see."

"Sure it will." He grinned, his grim expression disappearing. "Now let's go have lunch." He started the car. "There's a little café across the street from his restaurant. This time we can watch him in comfort."

Alex parked the Mercedes behind the small frame building and they entered through a side door. It was a charming place. Its small wooden tables were covered with bright yellow oilcloth, a bouquet of wild flowers in the center of each, and the most wonderful smells emanated from its back room. A lively trio of elderly musicians stood in the corner of the room, smiling happily as they filled the room with slightly off-key but enthusiastic music.

A few seconds after they had seated themselves at a window table a young, smiling waiter came over to take their order. He had the dark good looks that make the French so appealing, and while he waited for them to decide, he occupied himself by examining Kate's tight jeans with wide-eyed appreciation. There wasn't anything furtive about his observation and he showed such open, naïve pleasure in her natural endowments that Kate couldn't possibly feel offended.

She noticed, however, that Alex wasn't quite so complacent about accepting his admiration. He frowned and glared up at the young man and when he began to order his voice was stiff.

Glancing back to the menu, Kate tried to decipher the list. Then gradually she realized that Alex was talking too long to be ordering a meal. She raised her eyes as she caught a word or two of the rapid French Alex was using in his conversation with the waiter.

"*Épouse?*" she asked, placing a hand on his arm. "Doesn't that mean wife?" He smiled in satisfaction and she gasped. "Alex! Did you tell him we were married?"

There was no way she could let him get away with such a blatant lie. Kate caught the waiter's arm as he began to turn away and she started to stumble through a denial in her awful high school French.

The man gazed down at her, his eyes widening as she spoke, then he began to back away, shaking his head nervously as though she had threatened his life. She gazed after him for a moment, then turned her eyes to Alex in bewilderment. "What was that all about? Why—"

She broke off, growing even more confused when she took in his strangely mottled face.

"What were you trying to say?" Alex asked, his voice sounding choked.

"I wanted to say that you were telling him a big, fat lie." She stared at him, then asked warily, "Why? Isn't *canard* a lie?"

He shook his head abruptly, his large body shaking with laughter. He glanced at her to speak, then closed his mouth helplessly and shook his head again.

"What did I say?" Kate asked, sighing in resignation.

Alex visibly struggled to bring himself under control and said weakly, "You told him I was a giant duck."

"I—" She gasped, then remembered the look on the waiter's face. "He must think I'm crazy," she murmured.

She tried very hard to hold on to whatever remaining dignity she possessed, but she kept thinking of telling the man in very bad French that Alex was not only a duck but a giant duck. She did manage to moan in embarrassment as she began to laugh uncontrollably.

"It's all right, Duchess," he said, still chuckling. "Right now he's thanking the Lord that he didn't get saddled with a crazy wife."

Kate gave him a squelching stare and opened her mouth to let him know that the whole thing was his fault, but he stopped her before she got a word out.

"Our food," he said, indicating the nervous waiter who was returning to their table with a tray of appetizers.

Kate was hungry enough to let it go for the moment and she happily settled down to eat. After the appetizer, they feasted on a delicious lamb stew, thick with mushrooms and potatoes, accompanied by large, crusty rolls. The strawberry tarts they were served for dessert were topped with thick, fresh cream and absolutely melted in the mouth.

Every time the waiter brought another course they would end up red-faced as they tried to hide the laughter the wary teenager caused afresh. Once Kate had to kick Alex under the table when he very softly began to make a quacking sound.

She was mooning over espresso when Alex covered her hand with his.

"Listen," he said, smiling sweetly. "They're playing our song."

"We don't have a song," she grumbled, then turned her head toward the squeaky sound. The odd-looking trio had begun carrying their instruments—a tuba, an accordian, and a violin—from table to table, taking requests. Kate watched the bulging cheeks of the short, bald tuba player for a moment, then said, "What on earth are they playing anyway? I don't think I've ever heard it."

He turned toward them, his head cocked as he listened, then he nodded slowly in recognition. "It's 'Play That Funky Music,' " he said blandly.

Kate gave a shout of startled laughter, covering her mouth with her hand to keep from spraying him with wine. He was crazy! Wonderfully, wonderfully crazy, she thought as he picked up both her hands and his laughing eyes met hers. The kind of crazy she was beginning to feel it would be hard to live without.

Seven

After finishing their meal, Kate and Alex waited in the Mercedes for Alvarez to leave, then took up the chase once again. The road they now traveled was relatively flat, if a little rough, and the countryside was much greener than what they had left behind.

As they sped along, Kate watched sheep grazing in brilliant green meadows and occasionally she even got a glimpse of a shepherd, which thrilled her. Cowboys and ranch hands were familiar to her, but a real shepherd was a novelty and she regretted that she didn't have her camera. Of course, she thought with a wry smile, at the time she'd left Heather's house she'd thought the Oceanographic Museum would be the extent of her sightseeing. She hadn't exactly been prepared for a tour of the back roads of France.

"I've got it," Alex said suddenly, breaking into her reverie. "We haven't done 'Monster Mash' yet."

She smiled. Since lunch they had covered every song that existed in their combined repertoires, singing with exuberance if not total accuracy.

"There's a reason for that," she said, giving him a guileless look.

He stared straight ahead for a moment, his brow creased in thought. "I'm trying to decide if you're leading up to another insult," he said finally, then shrugged. "What the hell. I'm tough. Give it your best shot."

She gave him a "who me" look, hiding her smile. "We are not going to sing 'Monster Mash' because every imitation you do sounds the same . . . and it's impossible to harmonize with Willy Nelson doing Boris Karloff."

"Oh, yeah?" he said, darting an offended glance in her direction.

"I knew you'd respond with something pithy and to the point," she said, giving him an admiring glance. "Maybe I should write that down. How did you put that again? 'Oh, yeah'?"

"Oh, yeah?" he repeated with a chuckle. "And I suppose you think your Barbra Streisand was wonderful?"

"My—my Barbra—" she sputtered indignantly. "I'll have you know people come from all over Plum just to hear me sing 'Second Hand Rose.' "

"They're obviously Ethel Merman fans," he said, grinning broadly.

"You—you . . . Oh, yeah?" she got out finally as she turned sideways in her seat, preparing to carry the debate to the bitter end. Suddenly, though, she saw his facial muscles tense and glanced ahead in time to catch sight of a small goat darting into the road . . . and behind a boy giving chase.

Kate's breath caught in her throat as Alex

jerked on the steering wheel and the car veered sharply to the left. She kept her terrified eyes open long enough to see that they had missed the boy and the goat, but they were closed when she heard the final, sickening crunch.

"You okay, Katy?" he asked as she eased her eyes open.

She nodded, exhaling slowly. "How about you?"

He leaned back in the seat and closed his eyes briefly. "I'm all right, but I'm afraid the car is not."

The crunch she had heard. "What did we hit?"

"A boulder roughly the size of Mount Rushmore." He sighed and opened his door. "I guess I'd better stop putting it off and see what the damage is."

She got out of the car and joined him as he hunkered down beside the damaged fender. "Is it bad?"

"Bad enough, I'm afraid." He stood up, wiping his hands on his handkerchief. "The fender is buckled against the tire and the wheel is leaning at an odd angle."

"I guess we'll lose track of Alvarez now," she said, unaware of how regretful she sounded.

He leaned against the car and put his arm around her, pulling her against his side. "This means it's going to be tough even getting back to Monte Carlo. You've heard of the long walk? We may be making it together."

"Isn't there anything we can do?" she asked. "After all, we've trailed him for two days. It seems a shame just to give up now."

He studied her indignant face, a smile growing, then squeezed her tightly as though she had pleased him. "I'll walk back to those houses we passed a minute ago and see if I can get someone out here to tow the car in and take us home."

"Couldn't we get someone to bring us another car so we could go on?" she asked hopefully.

"By the time I get someone out here, our man will be long gone, I'm afraid." His hand pressed into her waist appreciatively. "But we gave it a good try, Katy." He kissed her on the forehead and began walking back the way they had come.

Kate watched him until he was out of sight, then sat down on a rock near the Mercedes. With her elbows propped on her knees, she thought about how she had fought him all the way, and now when she was going back she didn't want to. It felt unfinished. Not just Alvarez, but what was between them.

Thirty minutes later, she was beginning to get worried. It shouldn't have taken him this long just to make a phone call. Maybe the people living in the houses they had passed didn't own phones.

She stood and began to pace worriedly, then heard a muffled roar in the distance. The closer it drew, the more wary she became. When an ancient motorcycle pulled off the road and stopped beside her, she closed her eyes tightly, hoping against hope that it would go away.

But when she opened them again, it was still there and the driver now had the helmet under his arm and a wide grin on his face.

"Oh, no, Alex," she began, backing away. "Alex, I won't . . . I won't—"

"Come on, Duchess." He laughed, grabbing her arm to pull her forward. He placed a second helmet on her head and strapped it under the chin before she could stop him. "We'll lose him if we hang around any longer."

"What about the car?" she asked stubbornly. "We can't just leave it here."

"Paul's taking care of having the car towed back to a garage in that last village we passed." He climbed off to get her purse and his jacket from the backseat of the car. As he stowed them in a small compartment on the motorcycle, he said, "I thought we would be going back with him, but just as I was about to hang up the phone the son of the couple who own that little gray house pulled up. He was glad to sell this to me."

"Weren't we lucky," she muttered sarcastically. "Alex, I can't—I've never . . . and I'm not going to now," she added emphatically, but merely gave a low moan when he helped her climb on behind him.

"Why me?" she shrieked as the motor revved loudly and they pulled back onto the road. "When did I change lives with Penelope Pitstop? It's him," she said, tapping her helmet against his back. "He started it . . . and he's determined not to let it end until I'm dead or at least mangled beyond recognition."

"Did you say something?" he yelled over his shoulder.

"I was merely saying what a lovely day it was for being hit by a Mack truck."

He laughed and put on the speed. She hugged him tightly and suddenly found that it wasn't so bad. With her arms wrapped around his waist, she could feel the hard muscles of his back and stomach. The entire length of her body was pressed against his, letting his warmth invade her flesh in a way that was unbelievably erotic. When they left the quiet country road for the crowded freeway, the erotic warmth between them helped to keep her mind off the way the other drivers seemed to be bent on murder.

"Will we be able to catch him?" she shouted, raising herself slightly so her mouth was closer to his ear.

"I hope so, Duchess," he yelled back. "I certainly hope so."

For a while it looked as though they had lost him. Then, about thirty minutes after they had pulled onto the highway, they spotted the red Jaguar in the distance.

Once they had him in sight, Kate pressed her face tightly against Alex's back and kept her eyes closed to the cars and trucks that passed them at amazing speeds. She only opened them again when, quite a while later, Alvarez turned off the main highway. Staying a careful distance away, they followed him into Dijon. The stop-and-go city traffic was almost as bad as what they left behind, but at least they were keeping a less exciting pace.

When they stopped for a traffic signal, another, newer motorcycle pulled up beside them on the street. Kate loosened her grip on Alex and glanced over inquisitively. She almost did a double take, but luckily remembered her manners in time. However, she couldn't keep her eyes from widening as she gazed at them in awe.

"Alex," she hissed, reaching up to get close to his ear. "The most amazing people ride motorcycles. They keep staring at us . . . do you think they want us to join their gang?"

He chuckled and she saw him glance over at the couple beside them. The girl's hair was styled in a sort of long, spiky butch cut and she wore what looked like a mangled, thigh-length sweatshirt and high, tight leather boots . . . and apparently nothing else. Beautiful in spite of her strange haircut, with her large almond-shaped eyes and high cheekbones, she could have been a model.

After studying the girl's legs for an inordinate length of time, Alex turned away and murmured, "Nice bike."

Kate almost humphed in his ear, then, hearing his low chuckle, she poked him in the ribs instead and turned back to find herself the object of the unique girl's interest.

She was staring at them both with undisguised curiosity, her dark eyes drooping sensually. After a moment, she jerked her head toward Alex and asked in French, "Yours?"

Kate hesitated, then when she saw the way the girl was eyeing Alex, she shrugged and said, "Oui."

The girl said something Kate couldn't interpret literally, but she didn't really need a translation. "What a hunk" was universal.

Kate grinned, then glanced at the boy that the girl was glued to. His head was shaved smooth except for one thin, looped braid over his ear and his sweatshirt was similar to the girl's, except that perhaps it covered more of him.

"Yours?" Kate asked, also in French.

The girl laughed gaily, made a face as if to say "he's not much, but he's mine," then replied, "Oui."

When the light changed, both cycles began to pull away. Kate sent the dark-eyed beauty a farewell thumbs-up sign and they both laughed, understanding each other completely.

After Dijon, their course became more complicated. They followed one winding country road after another. Although there was not as much traffic, the road was rougher and Kate felt every bump on her derrière. The countryside continued to hold her interest. It was not something the average tourist would see on a trip to France and, although she was fully aware of the privilege, after a while she began to fear her legs would be permanently bowed.

I'm probably the only person in the world who'll go home from France with calluses on the inside of her thighs, she thought in resignation.

Kate began to laugh at the thought, then stopped abruptly as she looked up. One minute they were in the middle of nowhere, then suddenly they topped a hill and they landed directly in the center of a small country village. Alex slowed and began to maneuver the bike through the street crowded with vans and wagons.

"It must be market day," he called over his shoulder.

To avoid the crowd he pulled between two temporary produce stands that blocked the entrance to a side street. At the end of the small street, he slowed to turn east once again and all at once they were surrounded by a street full of costumed, laughing people.

"What's happening?" she asked in bewilderment, staring with wide-eyed amazement at the gaily decorated donkey directly in front of them.

He glanced over his shoulder, his eyes sparkling with laughter. "Unless I'm mistaken, we're trapped in a parade."

Kate glanced anxiously around at the crowd. Immediately behind them was what could only have been the high-school band. In front of the donkey was a horse-drawn wagon filled with waving children.

"You really know how to impress a girl, don't you?" she said loudly. "Do you often join parades?"

His laughter blended with the general merriment, and after a moment, Kate shrugged, then began to wave and throw kisses to the enthusiastic cheers of the spectators gathered at the side of the street.

She couldn't get used to the way these villages had been designed without sidewalks. The streets were barely wide enough to allow traffic and with the people gathered to watch the parade they were even narrower. The parade route took them past vividly painted shops with signs she couldn't interpret.

Eventually the procession came to a halt in a village square lined with crepe-paper-hung booths—booths filled with food of every imaginable kind and blocking every street except the one they had come in on.

Turning slightly, she saw the street behind them was filled with the band and band afficionados, making it very clear that they were indeed trapped.

Alex was surveying the place at the same time. After a moment, he shrugged, then looked down at her. "Come on, Duchess." He laughed. "Let's celebrate."

When they climbed off the motorcycle, food and drink were quickly thrust into their hands. For the next half hour the two of them ate and drank and slapped people on the back, raising their glasses in unending toasts with the friendly citizens of the farming village.

After upending her glass for the umpteenth time, Kate turned to Alex and whispered, "What are we celebrating?"

"Who knows?" he said, throwing an arm around her shoulder. "Could be a saint's day or simply the anniversary of a particularly good wine."

She shrugged. "I guess if Louisiana can have a festival celebrating poke salad, they can celebrate wine."

"Poke salad?"

"It's a vegetable that grows wild on the side of the road," she explained. "Kind of a cross between spinach and turnip greens. It looks really disgusting, but it doesn't taste bad. During the Depression lots of people in the South survived by eating poke salad."

When an elderly man approached Kate, speaking softly in French, Kate threw Alex a questioning glance.

"He wants you to dance," Alex said, smiling.

Kate curtsied her best curtsey, then swung out into the crowd on the arm of the surprisingly agile villager. She had no idea what type of dance they were executing, but she gave it all she had.

She returned breathless and laughing, only to be pulled back into the dance by Alex. The dancers and spectators acted as though Kate and Alex were according them a great honor by participating in their festival, waving and shouting encouragement as they danced past.

"Do you know what kind of dance we're supposed to be doing?" she asked breathlessly as they whirled around.

"Haven't the foggiest," he said with an unconcerned grin.

"I thought those people were yelling something like 'Nice of you to join us.' " She panted as they began to bounce exuberantly through a polka-like dance. "But they're probably commenting on the fact that neither of us knows what in the heck we're doing."

"The French admire courage," he said bracingly.

She started to comment, then suddenly remembered something as they slowed down to a waltz. "Alex, I forgot about Alvarez. How are we ever going to catch him? He's probably halfway across France by now."

He grinned and stretched himself to look over the crowd to their right. "Look."

Kate swiveled her head but could see only the celebrating farm people. Then the crowd parted for one brief instant and she spotted the red Jaguar at the side of the plaza, trapped as surely as they were. Behind the wheel, she glimpsed a dark man with sunglasses hiding most of his face. His exasperation was obvious as he scowled and tapped the steering wheel with impatient fingers.

Kate turned away, uneasy for a moment. But when she saw the look of satisfaction on Alex's face, she laughed and began concentrating once more on the dance.

The sun was hanging much lower in the sky before the crowds thinned enough for them to leave, and Kate was glad to have the suede jacket when they were on the road again. She was totally exhausted and beginning to think they would never stop when Alex slowed down and pulled the motorcycle over to the edge of the road.

"This is it," he said quietly.

Lifting her head from its resting place on his back, she looked around. They were on the top of a hill in the middle of nowhere. There wasn't even a side road in the vicinity. She opened her mouth to ask Alex what he meant when, down below them, she saw the red Jaguar. It had turned off the road and was on a long gravel drive. Kate caught her breath when she saw where the drive led.

It was a castle—or, more properly, a château. Rising above a small green river, gleaming white stone edifice, complete with turrets, was a copy in miniature of the châteaux she had seen in the Loire Valley. It even had the beautiful formal gardens containing intricate, manicured mazes.

Kate turned fascinated eyes to Alex and met a stiff, cold frown. "What's wrong?" she asked anxiously. "Do you know this place?"

He nodded shortly. "I went to school with Charles Sauset, the present owner," he murmured vaguely, his mind obviously on other things.

"The man who owns that went to school in Wisconsin?" she asked in confusion.

He inhaled slowly, shaking away the dark mood, then smiled down at her. "I'll explain it all to you as soon as we get to Paris," he said. "The important thing is that I called Charles along with a few other people that my friend who is being blackmailed and I went to university with. During the conversation I mentioned Alvarez . . . and Charles denied knowing him."

Why had he called people they went to the university with? she wondered, her curiosity burning. He said he would explain it all in Paris . . . Paris? "Why are we going to Paris?"

"A friend of mine has an apartment there that we can use while we figure out what to do."

She liked the way he included her in his calculations, as though he needed her help. She was too tired to wonder about how closely involved she had become with a man she had known for only two days.

He slowly turned the motorcycle and they began traveling back the way they had come until they reached a major road, then they turned northeast, heading for Paris.

It was dark when they reached their destination in a Parisian suburb and Kate had to force herself to stay awake. Alex parked the cycle and helped her off, then pulled her against him as they walked up the stairs that led to the second floor of a small brick building.

"You're exhausted," he said in concern.

"Nothing that three days of sleep or one glass of bourbon wouldn't cure," she said. "But how do you know your friend is going to be so eager to have us stay?"

"Pete is easy."

"Isn't Pete an odd name for a Parisian?"

"He's British and his name is actually Neville Petrie, but the last person who called him Neville is probably still recuperating." Alex chuckled.

"I thought you said he was easy?"

"About everything except his name. You should have seen him in school. He was crazy. His parents wanted him to go to Oxford, but he liked the personal freedom he found in France." He smiled. "I think Pete's crowning achievement came during our last year. With a Mardi Gras mask covering his face, he mooned the entire faculty at an afternoon tea."

"Ahead of his time, wasn't he? He sounds . . . interesting," she murmured. "I can't wait to meet him."

"He's settled down since then," he said as he rang the doorbell.

From the outside, the building looked undistinguished and even dreary. When the door was opened, though, Kate caught a glimpse of unashamed opulence before her eyes were drawn to the man who was hugging Alex with exuberance.

"Pete," Alex said, laughing as he turned to Kate, "this is Kate Sullivan and we're looking for a place to sleep."

"Katy, darling," the thin, elegant man said,

turning to hug Kate with even more enthusiasm than he had shown his friend. "My house is yours. My bed is yours." He looked down at her with raised eyebrows, then added, "Now that I think of it, my body is also yours. So when you get tired of this backward colonial, remember that."

"Yes—yes," she said in astonishment. "I will." Then as he ushered them inside, she murmured to Alex, "He's settled down, huh? I wish I could have met him in his prime."

"As you can see," Pete said, waving a hand toward several leather suitcases stacked beside the door, "I was on my way out. So you'll have the place to yourselves. I have an assignation in Marseilles. Very hush-hush, you understand." He chuckled lazily. "Her husband's a minor city official who wouldn't care if she slept with the entire fire department, but she likes a bit of intrigue."

He smiled and Kate suddenly realized that, although decidedly odd, he was a genuinely nice man. She wandered around the living room of the large apartment as Alex helped Pete with his bags. The furnishings matched their owner—elegant and a little offbeat.

Alex returned to the apartment and came up to stand behind her. "You know, if you take time to get to know him, he's really a good person, a man to trust."

"Did you think I was judging him?" she asked curiously.

"No, not really," he said, shrugging. "I just want you to like my friends."

"I do like him," she said sincerely. "He doesn't just smile with his mouth. His eyes smile too." She sighed. "Alex, I'd give next year's salary for a bath, but first I think I'd better call Heather."

"I have some calls to make, too, but they can

wait." He turned away and said over his shoulder, "I'll make sure there's food in the refrigerator while you call."

She made her call quickly, cutting off Heather's protests as soon as she managed to get a word in. She reassured her as best she could, then replaced the antique gold phone. Placing her hands in the small of her back, she stretched wearily, then went in search of Alex.

She found him still in the kitchen. "Heather thinks I'm a candidate for the Whoopee Wagon," she said, smiling as she walked into the room. "She insisted on repeating every single rumor she's ever heard about you."

He raised an eyebrow. "Were there any good ones?"

She shook her head. "Just the same dull stuff—wild women, drunken parties, weird sex."

"Weird sex?" He grinned. "Did she give you any details? I might want to write my autobiography someday."

She laughed, then gave him an inquiring glance. "Pete did say we should consider the place ours, didn't he?" When he nodded, she sighed. "Good. I'm going to start by considering the bathtub mine. I think some of those bugs that live in the hay decided to run away from home." Then she left him laughing in the kitchen.

Alex shook his head as she walked out, wanting to follow her, but knowing he had things to do. Besides, he reminded himself, he had promised he wouldn't push her.

He picked up the red wall phone and dialed his Monte Carlo number. He drummed his fingers impatiently on the counter as he waited for Paul to come on the line. When he did, Alex wasted no time in filling him in on the facts he and Kate had uncovered, then he listened without comment as Paul told him all that had happened at his end.

The conversation was short and Alex was just about to hang up when Paul said, "Still fascinated, boss?"

Alex didn't have to ask what he meant. "It's gone way beyond fascination. This is it, Paul. And if I have to hogtie her, she's coming back to Wisconsin with me."

Paul chuckled. "I never thought I'd see it happen." He was silent for a moment. "Just out of curiosity, what was it about her that made you know?"

"That I love her?" Alex asked slowly. He knew Paul's question wasn't idle curiosity. There was a woman back in the States that his friend had been dating for over a year and Paul still wasn't sure about their relationship.

"Thousands of people have tried to explain it," Alex said. "I don't know that I can do it any better than they did." He exhaled slowly. "She's the only woman I've ever met who knows all the words to both 'Surfin' Safari' and 'The Three Penny Opera.' She can laugh at herself . . . and at me." He paused and his voice was soft when he continued. "She's cocky and stubborn and sometimes a smartass, but she's also loyal and wise and brave. She . . . she—" How could he explain it? "She's just Kate," he finished with a shrug.

"I envy you," Paul said quietly. It was the first time Alex had heard that particular note in his voice—almost wistful.

After he hung up, Alex stood for a moment in silence, then shook his head and reached for the telephone again.

*   *   *

Kate stepped from the bathtub and wrapped a thick bath sheet around her dripping body. Pete's bathroom was almost as big as his bedroom. The tub, which resembled a small swimming pool, was set in a wooden platform two steps above the rest of the room. The steaming hot water had soaked away her tiredness and most of the aches. She felt ready for anything now.

Pulling a gaudy wine-colored robe from a brass rack, she slipped into it, then headed toward the kitchen.

When she saw Alex standing in front of the open kitchen door, she stared in amusement at what he was wearing. He had obviously taken a bath, too, for his dark hair was still wet and his feet were bare. He was wearing tight green designer jeans and a black T-shirt with a French obscenity hand-painted across the back.

"I see you borrowed from Pete too," she said, grinning broadly.

He glanced down at his clothes, then at the velvet robe that dragged the floor as she walked, and shook his head ruefully. "It's the only thing they couldn't teach him at school—taste." He raised one eyebrow. "On you, however, his stuff doesn't look bad." He gestured toward the table that held makings for sandwiches. "Are you hungry?"

She shook her head and sat down at the table. "I had enough at the festival to last several days, but you go ahead."

Joining her, he leaned back in his chair, resting his ankle on his knee lazily as he drank beer from a tall brown bottle. "We're invited to a party," he said, his eyes sparkling with excitement.

She caught her breath. "You called Sauset?" she asked.

He nodded. "He was thrilled to hear from me

again," he said dryly. "Of course, when I pressed for a meeting, he wasn't so thrilled. The best I could do was an invitation to his party tomorrow night." He paused. "Actually it might work out better this way."

She started to ask him what he meant, but his expression changed suddenly and she forgot all about Sauset. His brow was creased with worry lines and there was a brooding look about his eyes.

Something was definitely troubling him, and she was just beginning to wonder if he remembered she was in the room when he said without preamble, "Tony called Paul today. He got another letter." He shifted in his seat. "This is only the second one that's been delivered by mail. The others were all handed to him by Alvarez." He frowned. "I've always thought that was strange. It was as though he had to record Tony's reaction for someone else's pleasure."

He fell silent again, then said, "Tony and I were roommates in school."

"In college?"

"We shared an apartment in college along with Pete, but I'm talking about before that." He inhaled. "I have to go quite a ways back for you to understand the situation. My grandfather was François Denoisel Delanore, brother of the late Comte de Nuit." He smiled. "He was what you might call a black sheep. In 1912 he emigrated to America, bringing along just enough money to keep him in trouble. Then in 1916, when he was twenty-five, he met and married my grandmother. He settled down long enough to see my father born two years later, then he was killed in World War I. I can remember my grandmother talking about what a great hero he was for sacrificing his life for the country that had taken him in in his time of need." He grinned. "After she died, my father told me the old man had left Belgium just one step ahead of a bunch of irate husbands. He also told me the hero actually died in a barroom brawl. But it doesn't matter. She kept her dreams right up to the end."

He rested his forearms on the table as he continued. "What this is all leading up to is the fact that when I was twelve the old count was getting on in years and was—as they say—without issue. Dad had died when I was ten so the count got in touch with my mother. He eventually convinced her that since I could inherit the title at any time, I should be educated in the proper schools."

He picked up a piece of ham, staring ahead thoughtfully as he took a bite. "No one knew he would last as long as he did, but it probably wouldn't have made any difference. The right schools to him were European schools." He frowned, remembering. "So I went to France to boarding school. That's when I met Tony. Although his father was English, his French mother insisted his education be in French.

"The school wasn't bad, but can you imagine what it was like for a twelve-year-old kid who had never been out of Wisconsin before that?" He smiled, but it was a sad smile. "I was miserable. Tony was two years older, but had a maturity the English seem to breed into their children. He saved my life, Kate. He taught me how to take care of bullies without constantly getting my head bashed in. He was my brother, my friend, and I'm afraid sometimes my parent."

Kate had the feeling that there was more to it

than Tony taking care of him. He must have held on to Tony as his only family in a strange place.

"He also bailed me out of a French jail when I was fourteen," he said, grinning.

"The time you were in jail that doesn't count?" she asked, curiosity filling her eyes.

He nodded. "Henri, the boy who gave us a proper introduction the night we met, is having some trouble with his younger brother. That's why he knew about that time. I thought it would make him feel better."

"What happened?" she asked, studying his smiling face.

"When I think about it now, it seems it happened to another person. I had the crazy idea that if I got in trouble, my mother would let me come home. So I swiped a watch. Tony had his father take care of bailing me out and seeing that it didn't go on any permanent record." He glanced at her. "So you can see that I owe him quite a bit."

She nodded. Alex was a man who would pay his debts, no matter what the cost to himself.

"Later we both attended something called a *grande école*," he said. "I don't know if there's an American equivalent, but it's different from a university in that the students are prepared for high-ranking careers in such things as civil and military services, commerce, industry . . . things like that. Only about a tenth of all the students who try for it pass the entrance exams."

He shifted in his chair, then suddenly stood and began clearing the table, waving Kate away when she rose to help him.

"As unlikely as it seems," he went on, "that's where we met Pete . . . and Charles. I never really had anything against Charles. He just seemed a little odd to me." Deep lines appeared around his eyes as he concentrated on the past. "He would never participate. In anything. Sports, parties. Sometimes I wondered if he were participating in life. But he always watched those who did with an ugly jealousy." He shrugged as he put the last container in the refrigerator. "That's all I can tell you about Charles. He was there, but that's all. I haven't got a clue to why he's doing this to Tony. I can't remember him being any more resentful of Tony than of me or Pete.

"This . . . this incident that the letters keep referring to, it had nothing to do with Charles. No one was involved except Tony and a girl." He got another beer from the refrigerator and took a long swallow before going on with his story. "Her name was Hélène. She had short black hair that made her look like a mischievous boy until you looked closer. I have to admit I was a little in love with her myself . . . until I got to know her better." He shook his head. "I still can't understand how Tony could have been so thoroughly fooled by her. They were supposed to be engaged, but she kept the ring in her purse and only wore it when she was with Tony. She broke dates with him time after time and each time he made excuses for her."

"She was seeing someone else?"

"Someone else? There was an army of some-one elses. She even tried working her wiles on me once. But Tony was my friend and the fact that she was cheating on him made her look ugly. I wanted to tell Tony what I had seen and heard, but I felt it wasn't any of my business. You don't know how many times I've kicked myself for that."

"No, you were right," she said. "If he was obsessed with her, he wouldn't have believed you.

It would have caused a rift in your friendship at a time when he needed his friends."

He smiled at her attempt to ease his conscience, then shook his head. "One day she came to him and told him she was pregnant. Tony was over the moon. He liked children and it meant they would get married—which was what he wanted."

He drew in a harsh breath and she could tell the next part wouldn't be pleasant.

"She told him she didn't want the baby and she didn't want to get married," he said flatly. "All she wanted was enough money for an abortion. I could have killed her for that. She didn't even try to let him down easy. It was as though she enjoyed hurting him. Then when he refused to give her the money for an abortion, she changed her tune. She became sweet and pliant and talked about their future together. She said she hadn't really wanted to get rid of the baby; she was only testing him, to see if he really loved her or would take the easy way out." He sighed. "You can guess what happened then."

"She pretended to need money for something else?" she asked quietly.

"For prenatal care," he confirmed in disgust. "She could have let it go at that. She could have simply told him later that she had miscarried. But she didn't. She called him the next day to tell him she was on her way to an abortionist and that he didn't have to worry about it because the baby wasn't his."

She sucked in her breath. "A double blow," she whispered with the sheen of unshed tears glistening in her eyes. "Losing her and the baby at the same time."

He nodded. "Tony went crazy. I tried to stop

him, but there was nothing I could do except trail along behind as he went through the slums looking for her. He didn't even know what part of town she was in when she called. When I finally convinced him it was impossible to find her, we went back to the apartment and sat up all night waiting for her to call again."

He paused and she knew she didn't want to hear what he was going to say next.

"The police called about nine the next morning," he said quietly. "They had found his telephone number in Hélène's purse. She was dead. She had bled to death in a little room in a suburb of Paris."

She tried to take in all he had told her, but it was too much, too fast. "I'm sorry, Alex," she said, her voice hoarse. She covered both his hands with hers. "It must have been very painful for him." *And you,* she added silently. *The friend who wanted so badly to comfort but couldn't.*

They sat for a while as they were, hands entwined, communicating silently. Then Kate said, "But I still don't understand about the blackmail part, Alex. The only guilty party is dead. How could anyone threaten Tony with that kind of information?"

"I've tried to tell him that," he said, nodding. "The letters blame him for everything—the pregnancy, the abortion, and Hélène's death—but he had nothing to do with any of it."

She rubbed her forehead thoughtfully. "Was his affair with Hélène common knowledge?"

"In our circle? Sure it was. But everyone also knew Hélène was sleeping around. No one connected her death with Tony."

"Someone obviously did . . . and still does. They're out to hurt him." She glanced at him. "I suppose the notoriety that would follow newspaper stories would do that."

"In his profession, notoriety is the norm." When she glanced at him in inquiry, he said, "Have you ever heard of Anthony Blakewell?"

She started to shake her head no, then stopped. "Anthony Blakewell . . . the Shakespearean actor?"

He nodded. "No, it's not publicity that's bothering him. Or the threats to tell his wife. Diane knows all about it. What's throwing him is that the author of those letters claims to have evidence that the baby was Tony's after all." He hesitated. "Tony and Diane can't have children. I think that's part of what's eating at him. He simply wants to know the truth and he wants the constant reminders to stop. He wants the past to be buried for good."

"What exactly do the letters say?"

"After accusing Tony, they demand that he turn down a contract he's been offered—the chance to star in a movie. It would mean a move to California, but it could be a major break in his career. He won't give that up. And even if he were willing, it wouldn't get him any closer to the truth. The only way is to find out who's sending them and why." He frowned, flexing his shoulders wearily. "And that's where I come in. I've got to find out who it is and stop him."

"*We've* got to," she corrected him softly.

"That's right," he said, the tired look disappearing from his eyes as he gazed at her. "Did I tell you how lovely you look in Pete's robe?"

She grinned, trying to copy his light tone. "Pete's got rather flamboyant taste, doesn't he?"

"It matches his personality," he said dryly.

He stood and stretched, his strong, lean body holding her eyes fast. When he turned and found her eyes on him, he caught his breath sharply. Then, shaking his head, he said, "I guess we'd better decide where we're going to sleep, Duchess."

She nodded silently and followed him out into the hall. They were both avoiding the sensual tension that had been building steadily. Being alone in an apartment was suggestive enough without this thing, this incredible awareness, that was between them.

"Would you rather have Pete's bedroom or the guest room?" he called back over his shoulder.

"I think I'd prefer the guest room. Pete looks like the type to have concealed mirrors over the bed."

He laughed. "Not that I know of, but I wouldn't swear to it." He opened a door and showed her a modest-sized bedroom, elegant in powder blue and gray but not as showy as the rest of the apartment. Its small satin-covered bed was obviously built for one and she stared at it for a moment.

She hesitated as she walked through the door, glancing up at him through her lashes. "I guess I'll see you in the morning then," she said huskily.

He nodded and started to turn away, then halted abruptly and swung back around and pulled her into his arms.

"Kissing in bedroom doorways can be dangerous stuff, Katy," he whispered. "But I'll be damned if I can wait till we're in a more circumspect place."

He dipped his head and pressed his lips against hers, lightly at first, but within seconds he lost control and the kiss showed his fierce need. Kate didn't even try to withstand the onslaught. She had been aching for this kiss all day— ever since she had found him kneeling beside her in the hay that morning. She parted her lips eagerly, meeting his searching tongue with her own.

Last night she had stopped him because her feelings for him were confused. Tonight there was no confusion, no hesitation. Her path was clear-cut . . . and it led straight to him.

The kiss deepened until she felt they were merging into one. Her hands climbed up his back beneath his T-shirt, her fingers grasping and kneading the hard muscles. She felt him tremble at her touch and a thrill such as she had never felt coursed through her.

When he reached inside the velvet robe and took the weight of one breast in his callused hand, she felt fire leaping in her blood and raised her knee to press her bare thigh against his. He was pressing her back into the doorjamb urgently and with his free hand he cupped her buttock to bring her closer as the fever burned in them both.

He drew back his head with stiff abruptness, sucking in a harsh gasp of breath. His hand shook slightly as he gently stroked her cheek and stared into her caramel-colored eyes.

"I'm not rushing you, am I, Katy?" he rasped out urgently.

"*No,*" she said, giving a shaky laugh.

"Good." The word came out in a gust as he took her hand, and she blinked in surprise when he began to pull her with rough haste toward the master bedroom.

As they went through the door, she smiled indulgently at the relief she had heard in his voice. The heat between them had been banked down to a slow boil now that they were no longer locked in each other's arms, and she was pleased to see that there was none of the embarrassment that people usually feel after having exposed their emotions to another.

"I'm so glad you're not shy, Katy," he said, echoing her thoughts as he closed the door behind them. "Because I can't take it slow and romantic. Not now. Not when I've been waiting so long for you."

"Two days?" she asked, giving him a slow smile.

"Not two days—thirty-seven years," he corrected softly. "All my life I've been waiting for you, Katy. I always knew you existed; I just didn't know where to find you." He inhaled a short, exuberant breath. "Oh, Duchess, I have so many things to show you."

"Oh?" she murmured, her brows raised as he stripped off his T-shirt.

"No," he said, laughing. "I mean other things. When I would come across a particularly spectacular view back in Wisconsin, I used to think, 'She should be here with me to see this.' " He gathered her close again. "I even bought you things. Do you think that's strange? When I would find something—a piece of porcelain or a pen-and-ink drawing—that was too exquisite to pass by, I would buy it and put it away, telling myself, 'This is for her.' "

"No," she whispered hoarsely. "I don't think that's strange. I think it's the loveliest thing I've ever heard." He had told her once that he wasn't romantic. Someday she would have to correct that misconception. Someday, but not now.

He tossed his T-shirt on a chair, then pulled her into his arms again as though he couldn't stay away even for the time it took to remove the rest of his clothes.

"You feel it, too, don't you, Katy?" he whispered hoarsely as he spread the lapels of the robe and ran his open hand over her taut nipples. "You feel the inevitability of it . . . of us being together. Our bodies fit together the same way our minds do. Two pieces of a two-piece puzzle. We connect where we're supposed to connect."

She moaned and arched her upper body, needing to feel his hot flesh against hers. The rough hair of his chest abraded the sensitive tips of her breasts as she pushed closer and rubbed against him, sending a fiery streak of pleasure straight to her core.

Her robe had already slipped to the floor and together they somehow managed to remove the rest of his clothes before they walked to the bed. As she sat on the side of the bed, he undid her braid and she heard him moan deep in his throat as he pulled her back and wrapped her hair around them both.

Moments later, as he leaned over her and murmured softly, Alex touched every part of her body. Not with the sure, slick touch of a practiced lover, but as though he were discovering a new world.

The wonder and breathless joy she saw on his face were more exciting, more erotic than anything she had ever imagined and she reacted with the same open wonder as she ran her hands over his hard male form.

It was only when the pleasure grew too intense for them to endure that they came together with a passionate fierceness, a piercing joy. His rough breathing and hoarsely spoken words of love brought her quickly to the place she sought with her arching hips. As he thrust deeply, she met the stroke and felt a blinding burst of uncontrollable pleasure that shook her body in waves. She dug her fingers into his back as she felt his body shudder in the *grand frisson* and knew that he had found his release too.

For long moments.the silence was broken only by the harsh sound of their labored breath. Then, as though their joint physical release had brought about a similar release in their minds, they began to talk quietly, about life, about love, and about themselves, sharing things they had never shared with another human being.

The darkness was beginning to glow faintly in a prelude to dawn when they fell asleep with their weary bodies entwined.

Eight

Kate poked her head around the curtain and saw Alex relaxing on an elegant floral sofa in the salon of the dress shop they had entered thirty minutes earlier. Drawing in a final bracing breath, she thrust aside the curtain and stepped out into the room.

He didn't see her until she strolled in an exaggerated model's walk onto the show floor in front of him. Then he leaned back lazily, his fingers forming a peak as he rested his hands on his stomach.

She was dressed in deep emerald green satin knickers, a pale lilac gauzy blouse with voluminous sleeves, and a pert sequined green hat with a flirty little veil just barely covering her eyes. Except for the hat, she could have been one of the Three Musketeers.

Alex ran his eyes up and down her flamboyant costume, then murmured, "You've got to have it, Duchess."

Turning his head, he nodded to the attentive saleswoman standing behind him, but while his back was turned, Kate waved frantically at the woman, shaking her head in an emphatic negative motion.

They had already chosen her dress for this evening. It was a floor-length sheath of dusty green silk jersey that they had found in a little shop earlier. Its halter top had pearl buttons that ran from throat to waist, allowing the dress to be as demure or provocative as the wearer wished.

The dress and accessories were stored away in the trunk of the Renault Alex had rented, along with the things he had purchased for himself. Now they were simply having fun.

Shopping in Paris was unlike anything she had ever experienced before and Kate knew the two of them were behaving like children in a toy store, but she didn't care. She had heard all her life that Paris was for lovers and today she and Alex were proving it.

She had never known a man who liked shopping, but Alex liked hats . . . any kind of hat. And he liked to watch as Kate tried them on. So she had tried on hats. Dozens of hats. She had tried on enough hats to last her a lifetime. Hats that looked like flying saucers with brims big enough to shade the whole town of Plum, and hats as small as teacups. She had tried on feathered hats and beaded hats, outrageous hats and demure hats.

And she had posed and postured before a laughing Alex who had urged her to buy everything she tried on. After a while she realized it was a losing battle and stopped arguing with him, simply canceling his orders when his back was turned, as she had just done.

As soon as she had changed, she rushed him out of the shop before he could discover that she had canceled the order for the knickers. She had bought enough casual clothes to last her a couple of days and she refused to let him spend his money on her.

He found it hard to understand why she wouldn't accept his gifts as naturally as she accepted his body and his friendship, but she had been paying her own way for a long time and remained steadfast in her refusal.

And remaining steadfast with Alex was not an easy task, she thought later that evening as she dressed for Sauset's party. When he gazed down at her with loving eyes, everything solid in her body turned to liquid.

She smiled as she thought of the way he had looked that morning when he woke to find her leaning over him, studying his features. The look on his face was the most touching thing she had ever seen. As incongruous as it sounded, there had been an innocence about the look he had given her, like a child who had just seen his first bluebird. And as she stared down at him, her heart had almost burst with love.

Oh, yes, she loved him. She had known that even before they made love. Somewhere on their wild trip from Monte Carlo, somewhere on that ridiculous motorcycle or on a pile of hay, she had fallen deeply, irrevocably, in love and the wonder of it filled her completely.

She stared at her sparkling eyes in the mirror of Pete's bathroom and smiled slowly, then began to put the last touches of makeup on her face. She fingered one of the wispy curls that lay against her face, setting off the Gibson Girl look that had been adapted for her long hair, then shook her head and began to apply a beige, almost invisible lipstick.

Giving her hair a final pat, she picked up her evening bag and stepped out of the dressing-room, then stopped abruptly as Alex turned around. It was the first time she had ever seen him in evening dress and the sight took her breath away.

The noble savage, she thought as her eyes roamed hungrily over his now familiar lines.

"You're gorgeous," she said, then her gaze returned to his face, and the look in his eyes as he stared at her pulled her across the room and into his arms.

"Men aren't gorgeous," he said huskily. "I'm only breathtakingly handsome; you're gorgeous." He dipped his head to kiss her and she had no chance to answer as the kiss took every thought from her head.

"We really have to go to this thing, don't we?" he murmured a few minutes later against her throat while his fingers kneaded her buttocks and pressed her close.

"Uh-huh." Her reply came out in a breathless whisper and she felt his hands tighten their hold.

He inhaled roughly. "Okay, the sooner we get it over with, the sooner we can come back here." He grasped her arm and began to urge her toward the living room. "Come on," he said grimly. "Let's get on with it."

He stopped suddenly by the front door and pulled something from his coat pocket, extending it toward her.

"What is it?" she asked, glancing down at the thin black cylinder.

"It's a penlight."

"Sure it is." She took it from him and stood for a moment staring at it in bewilderment. "Alex, do I want to know why I need a penlight at a party?"

He laughed at her wary tone. "Just in case we get a chance to do some sleuthing."

"Sleuthing?" she murmured. Then excitement began to grow in her brown eyes. "You mean I get to help?"

He pulled her to his side and moved across the room to the front door, his arm thrown around her shoulders. "You've been with me since the beginning of this chase," he said, his fingers pressing into her side as he spoke. "I figured you'd want to be in at the kill."

"Never say kill to a coward," she said, pushing her face against his pleated silk shirt. "Actually," she added, pulling back to stare at him, "I guess it's a kind of compliment that you trust me enough to let me help you."

He smiled. Then as they walked through the door, he said softly, "I would trust you with my life, Duchess, without a minute's hesitation."

When they were settled in the rented Renault, she placed the slender flashlight in the bottom of her bag, checking carefully to make sure there were no suspicious bulges. She tried to think of the evening ahead, but his last words kept echoing in her mind.

He trusted her. With his life he trusted her. This was the relationship that she had been dreading, she realized with surprise. She depended on another human being for her happiness . . . and more—she was willing to do anything in her power to make him happy.

She smiled, unconcerned that all of Evan's predictions had come true. She would have to bring Heather's husband a gift when she saw him. Because he had been right. Alex had given her more than anyone in her life and, in return, she could hold back nothing from him.

Moments later, Kate glanced out the window and realized with surprise that they had arrived at the château. She smoothed down her dress nervously as Alex pulled the rented car into the long driveway.

She hadn't been at all nervous when they had shopped for evening clothes, or even when she had been carefully applying her makeup. But now that they had actually arrived at their destination, butterflies were fluttering frantically in her stomach.

When they entered the large, marble-tiled entry hall she felt as though everyone present were staring at the faint crease at the bottom of the little gold purse.

The château might have been small compared to the ones in the Loire Valley, but to her it looked like the real thing. It was filled with furniture she had only seen in books and museums and had wall hangings as big as her cabin in Plum, rising all the way to the second floor. She would have loved to stop and examine the smaller, more intricate tapestries, but she kept her mind firmly on why she and Alex were attending this party.

They walked through a doorway and the low roar of voices and music washed over them in oscillating waves. The grand salon of the château was full to overflowing, and Kate smiled at everything that moved in an attempt to act naturally.

Alex cast his eyes around the room, searching for Sauset, but in the press of wall-to-wall flesh it was impossible to find an individual one wanted to find.

He glanced down at Kate. Lord, she was lovely. Almost as lovely as she had been when he had awakened that morning. For a moment he thought he had dreamed her, but only for a moment. The warm flesh pressing against his had convinced him that she was real.

He shook his head, forcing his mind back to the business at hand. "Duchess," he said, leaning down so she could hear him. "I'm going to search for our host. Stay right here by this wall hanging so I can find you when I come back."

"What am I supposed to do while you're gone?" she asked dryly, gazing up at him.

Alex smiled. She sounded nervous. "What do you usually do at a party? You laugh at stupid jokes and admire ostentatious jewelry. You discuss in minute detail the latest diet and the 'in' malady and this month's favorite ski resort. . . . What are you looking for?" he asked as she opened her bag and began to peer inside.

"A pad and pencil," she said dryly. "I think I'd better take notes."

He laughed and gave her a quick kiss on the nose. "Just be yourself. I won't be gone long."

He moved slowly through the clusters of people, occasionally glancing over his shoulder to see how Kate was doing. He hadn't gotten very far before he saw her being cornered by a couturier he had met several times.

He stifled a grin. Poor Kate. The man was one of the world's greatest bores.

Shifting his gaze forward again, he stiffened when he saw Sauset at the center of a group of people on his right. He headed in that direction and could tell the minute his host spotted him. Sauset's features became harsh for a split second before he smiled in delight.

"Alexandre," he said heartily, extending his

hand as Alex drew nearer. "So glad you could make it. It's a pleasure seeing you again."

He began introducing the newcomer to the guests around him, and, through half-closed eyes, Alex observed him closely. Sauset was agitated about something; that much was obvious. There was something feverish in his attempted heartiness.

"You're looking well, Charles," Alex said when there was a break in the conversation.

"And you, Alex. Or perhaps I should say Comte de Nuit," he returned. "You're even browner than you were in university. I always thought you looked a little barbaric." He laughed as though it were a great joke. "But it was a barbarism that certainly didn't hurt your popularity with the opposite sex." He glanced around curiously. "I thought you were bringing a friend. Surely you didn't come alone?"

"No," he said, watching a faint sheen of perspiration form on Sauset's forehead as he continued to stare at him. "I came with a very special lady. She's waiting across the room for me."

"But you should bring her over," he enthused. "I must meet this special lady."

Nodding stiffly, Alex moved away. When the crowd closed around him, he stopped beside a potted palm and turned to watch Sauset. What did he have against Tony? Why was he determined to make him suffer? Alex cast his mind back over their school days, but couldn't find a clue to what was happening now. As far as he knew, Charles had never even met Hélène. So why now was he digging up such a sad episode from the past?

Kate moved slowly through the laughing crowd, her eyes scanning the room continuously. She hoped she hadn't missed Alex somewhere along the way, but she had no intention of spending the evening in conversation with a barnacle.

Suddenly she spotted him and moved quickly to the other side of the palm. Parting the branches, she leaned closer and said huskily, "Hiya, sailor. Got a match?"

Alex jerked his head around and smiled at her through the palm leaves. "Hello, Duchess," he said, reaching through to pull her around next to him. "I was just coming to get you."

"Yes, I can see you were," she murmured sourly. "I must say, it's about time," she whispered, giving him a vengeful look. "Skulduggery I was prepared for, but you didn't tell me I would be bored to death."

"Bored?" he asked, raising one heavy eyebrow. "But Mario is a renowned wit."

"The man is monosyllabic," she insisted dryly. "My eyes kept crossing." She glanced up at him. "So what did you find out? Do you think Sauset is the one?"

"I didn't find out anything," he murmured. "But yes, I think it's he. He wants to meet you."

"Should I be flattered?" she asked as they began to make their way back across the room, then she smiled up at him. "I did some investigating while you were gone."

"Did you?" He glanced down at her in inquiry. "What did you find out?"

"I found out that I definitely can't speak French, Italian, or Swahili. I tried to question the maid, but she kept directing me to the ladies' room. And there's a very regal-looking black man over there who spent ten minutes looking at me like I was something in a petri dish . . . makes me wonder what I asked him," she added wryly.

Alex grinned, then suddenly his hand tightened painfully on her arm. "Alvarez," he said, indicating a man who was taking a glass of champagne
from a passing waiter.

It was the first time she had seen the man in
the red Jaguar close up and Kate studied him
surreptitiously, then stood up on tiptoes to whisper, "He looks like Peter Lorre playing one of Sir
Laurence Olivier's parts."

Alex gave a short laugh. "I wonder if Charles
will still deny knowing him."

When at last they stood beside their host it
seemed Alex wasn't willing to waste time finding
out. As soon as he had introduced Kate, he said
bluntly, "I saw Alvarez, Charles. I thought you
said you didn't know him."

Sauset's features tightened. "Really, Alex.
You're like a dog with a bone. I don't know this
person to whom you constantly refer. If he is here,
another guest must have brought him along. I
certainly didn't invite him." He turned to Kate
and smiled brilliantly. "I'm sure Miss Sullivan isn't
interested in this boring man."

Kate studied the man's features carefully. He
didn't look like a blackmailer. He looked slightly
petulant, but attractive nonetheless—certainly not
evil.

She returned his smile pleasantly. "On the
contrary," she said. "He looked like an extremely
interesting man." She gave Alex a naïve glance.
"Maybe we should ask Mr. Alvarez how he came to
be here?"

Alex's eyes gleamed with hidden laughter.
"Maybe we should at that."

By unspoken agreement, they nodded to Sauset
and began to move away. They spotted Alvarez

immediately, but he was deep in conversation with an auburn-haired woman.

"Charles is guilty as hell, Katy," Alex said. "I can feel it in my bones."

She stared silently at Alex for a moment. "So what do we do now?" she asked. "You don't really think Alvarez will tell us anything, do you?"

"Not a chance. We're going to have to search the place and try to come up with some evidence." He remained silent for a moment as he stared out into the crowd. "He's watching us like a hawk. I think you're going to have to distract him, Duchess, so he won't see me slip out."

"Distract him?" She nibbled on a manicured nail as she considered the suggestion, then, reaching down, she slipped two buttons on her dress free. Drawing in a deep breath in an effort to show more cleavage, she nodded her head. "Distract him," she repeated emphatically.

Alex grabbed her arm as she began to move away, glancing down at her with a frown, then he quickly refastened the buttons. "Like I said, *we'll* wait for someone to distract him, then *we'll* slip out."

Kate smiled at the look in his eyes and shrugged. For the next fifteen minutes they stood at the edge of the room, trying very hard to look like average party-goers. Then, as though ordered to do so, a blond woman cornered Sauset, maneuvering him into a corner behind a marble statue.

"Now let's go," Alex said.

They moved unobtrusively toward the door, stopping occasionally to speak to people they passed, behaving as if they were merely mingling. Then, keeping a careful eye on Sauset and Alvarez, they slipped through the arched doorway into the adjoining entry hall.

The other guests were moving around freely so no one noticed as Alex and Kate climbed the wide marble staircase. When they gained the next landing they turned right and Alex halted before the first door.

Checking both ends of the hall, he slowly eased the door open. The room was dark and Kate couldn't tell if it was the one they were looking for. She started to move forward, but a creaking noise stopped her. As Alex hastily closed the door, she caught a glimpse of the couple on the bed.

"Wrong room," he whispered with a grin, and began moving to the next door.

She glanced back over her shoulder at the closed door. "You'd think they would have at least locked the door," she hissed, moving to stand behind him.

The next room was luckily empty, but it was too feminine to be the master bedroom so they left it behind. The third door he tried seemed to be the right one. By the light coming from the hall they could see a masculine-looking dark satin robe lying on the end of a huge four-poster bed.

"This looks like it," he said quietly as they moved together into the room.

Kate gasped as the door closed behind them, throwing the room into deep darkness. "Why can't we turn on the light?" she whispered when she saw the thin stream of light from his flashlight.

"I saw guards outside when we pulled up." He moved farther into the room. "They might ignore a light in here, but I don't want to take any chances," he said over his shoulder as he pulled open the drawer of a small desk.

Her eyes began to adjust to the dark and she fished the other penlight out of her bag. Moving to a delicate antique bedside table, she pulled out the small drawer and directed the light into its interior. She could hear Alex searching a bureau as she quickly rifled through the contents of the drawer. She found a rather racy paperback novel and a handful of old photos, but no letters.

Next she opened a small trunk, but it must have been purely ornamental for it was empty. Moving slowly around her side of the room, she examined each drawer and several small boxes. She even stopped to check the bottoms of the drawers because she had seen it done once on a detective show, but she found nothing of interest.

Kate thought she had reached a dead end until, in the dim light, her eyes picked out a door to her right. Expecting to find nothing more than the bathroom, she reached out and tried the knob, then drew in a triumphant breath when she found it locked.

Shining the light into her purse, she looked quickly through her credit-card case and finally pulled out her thin, flexible library card. Holding her breath, she slid it carefully in next to the lock.

"Son of a gun," she murmured in surprise as the door opened. "It actually works."

She ran the thin stream of light over the contents of the closet, then stopped, a bewildered look crossing her expressive features before she examined the peculiar things in the closet again.

"Alex?" she whispered, her voice puzzled.

"I can't find anything in here except a lot of monogrammed underwear," he said in disgust. "Even if he isn't our blackmailer, I couldn't ever like a man who wore designer jockey shorts. He—"

"Alex," she said again, interrupting his muttering. "I think Sauset is a little strange. He has rows and rows of elaborate leather belts. And that's not all. I recognize the whip and the chains, but what is that—"

Alex came up behind her and pulled her out of the closet, closing the door firmly behind them.

"But I wasn't through checking," she protested, trying to disengage her arm.

"You're through," he said emphatically as he urged her away from the closet.

She stopped struggling and studied his face for a moment. "You're not going to tell me what that thing on the top shelf was, are you? It looked like a giant—"

"Kate, we aren't here to explore the sexual preferences of the man," he said firmly. "We just want to find out what he's using to blackmail Tony."

"Sexual? That stuff was sexual?" She shook her head, then muttered ruefully, "I gotta get out more."

He started to laugh, then stopped abruptly and pulled her into his arms.

"What in—"

Her protest was smothered by his lips just as the door swung open. "I beg your *pardon*," said an embarrassed voice, then the door closed quietly.

But Kate and Alex didn't notice. They were still involved in the kiss. It was several minutes later before she spoke. "Alex," she whispered huskily as his lips began to trail down her throat. "He's gone."

"Who's gone?"

She gave a breathless laugh, rubbed her cheek against his, and slipped her arms inside his jacket.

"Kate . . . Kate, I think we'd better leave now," he whispered hoarsely as she massaged the muscles of his back. "That bed gets closer every time I look at it."

He made a rough sound, then released her. Moving to the door, he opened it enough to look out, then motioned for her to follow him.

"Now his study," he said, running a hand over his hair to smooth it down.

"Do you know where it is?" she asked.

Kate held her skirt up with one hand as they moved back down the staircase. As they walked, she looked around the large hall. It seemed strange to find the party going on just as they had left it.

"Tony and I visited Charles once when we were at school," he said, his brow creased in thought. "It was right after we met him . . . before we found out how odd he was. But that was a long time ago. I hope I can still find it."

He led her to the hall that ran beneath the staircase, then seemed to get his bearings. They stood in front of the door he had decided on and talked quietly until the hall was clear of people, then stepped inside quickly, relieved to find his memory was correct.

"If it's here, it will most likely be in his desk." He closed the door behind them and Kate once again dug the flashlight out of her purse. While he rifled through the desk, she moved around the room shining the thin stream of light to the right and left as she walked.

She would have been better off had she directed the flashlight straight ahead for suddenly the light swung wildly to the ceiling and there was a muffled crash as she landed in a heap on the floor.

"Duchess," he hissed. "Is that you?"

"No, it's Irving Schwartz," she said sarcastically. "Of course it's me."

He had started toward her in concern as soon

as he heard the noise, but now there was laughter in his voice as he asked, "What happened?"

"I tripped over a—" She stopped and felt the large object that was presently beneath her knees, then drew back her head with a gasp when she felt its hairy surface. "Oh, Lord, it's—it's"—she fumbled around on the floor until she found the penlight, then directed its light at the thing tangled up in her long legs—"it's a stupid stuffed bobcat or something," she said in disgust.

When Alex reached her, he bent to help her up. "Why aren't you wearing your glasses?" he asked, chuckling as she kicked out at the stuffed cat that had tripped her. "You know you can't see two feet without them."

"I'm not wearing them because—" she began irritably, then she stopped abruptly as he grasped her arm and jerked her across the room after him.

Alex had managed to shove her behind a curtain and up onto the window seat, but not join her himself before the door opened and the light was switched on. Kate held her breath as she pressed her body flat against the massive diamond-paned window. She could do nothing but bite her lip and wait silently for Alex to be discovered. So she waited . . . and waited, but nothing happened.

Somehow he must have hidden himself after he had hidden her. She glanced behind her into the dark night and wondered if she was visible from outside, then someone spoke and startled her back to awareness of their danger.

"Close the door."

The voice was Sauset's and it was no longer pleasant. It was low and stiff with anger, causing a cold shiver to run through her body. She forced herself to remain still, even controlling her breathing as he continued.

"I told you not to come here tonight." He stopped and made a choking sound of rage. "Go ahead and smile," he hissed. "See if you are still smiling when I refuse to give you your last payment."

"Now, Charles," a placating voice said. It had to be Alvarez. Kate had never heard him speak, but it couldn't be anyone else. She didn't like his voice; it sounded oily and unpleasant.

She could hear them moving around, and being unable to see what was happening was driving her crazy. She had to know where Alex was and if he were well hidden.

Easing sideways, she moved an inch at a time to reach the division in the curtains where slivers of light streamed into her hideaway. She not only had to make sure no part of her body disturbed the curtains, she had to move slowly enough that she didn't stir the air in the alcove. Steadily she moved. One more inch and she was there.

She lifted her eyes from her feet and stared through the slight gap . . . at the back of a man's head. Swallowing her terrified gasp, she became a statue for the long seconds that followed. It seemed like years later when he finally moved away and continued speaking.

"There was no harm done," Alvarez said pleasantly, apparently not sensing Kate's presence. "What can he do, for heaven's sake?"

"I don't like it, damn you," Sauset spat out quickly, his face livid. "He's up to something. If you hadn't come, he would have been helpless. He might have suspected, but he could have proved nothing."

Kate cast her eyes about the room frantically,

but could find no hint of Alex's presence. That was good, she assured herself. If she couldn't see him, then they couldn't see him. She didn't want to think about the fact that she wasn't wearing her glasses and couldn't see clearly even the men in the middle of the room. She just wanted to believe that Alex was safe. She had to believe it.

Then suddenly something caught her attention and she stiffened in alertness. It wasn't much, just a slight movement under the sofa that caught her eye, but she was convinced it was Alex. Although she kept her gaze on the same spot, she could detect no further movement.

"He can prove nothing now," Alvarez said casually, then laughed. "He is like a flea to a dog. Annoying, but inevitable and harmless."

"You grow too sure of yourself, René. I won't have that *bourgeois* interfering with my affairs." He inhaled roughly and Kate could see his hand slapping against his thigh impatiently. "I wanted to play out the ending, to handle it with finesse, but it can't be done now."

Alvarez had been moving about the room restlessly as Sauset spoke. For a moment he paused beside the leather sofa and Kate held her breath when he pulled up his trouser legs and bent to sit down. Kate began to tremble as he crossed his legs and threw his arm over the back.

"I shall make the final move now," Sauset continued as he walked toward his desk. "I want you to go to the cottage and wait for me."

"Now?" Alvarez stood up suddenly and Kate sagged in relief as he moved toward Sauset. "It would be my pleasure, of course. However, I'm afraid I have plans."

"But you'll cancel them, won't you, my dear René?" Sauset's voice was smooth and deadly as he turned away to pick up something from the desk.

For a moment, silence filled the room, then Alvarez laughed shortly. "Yes, I believe I will."

"Then go. I'll slip away as soon as I can manage it." They walked single file to the door, then as Sauset pulled it open, he turned back and said, "And René . . ." He paused and at that moment Kate's purse slipped from her trembling fingers, hitting the padded window seat with a thump that echoed like a gunshot in her ears.

She stood rigid with her eyes closed, waiting breathlessly for the curtain to be jerked aside.

". . . you had better be there," Sauset said softly.

Then the room was once more in darkness and she heard the door close with a soft thud.

Nine

Kate slumped back against the window, then, shaking her head, she parted the curtain and stepped down. She picked up her purse and stared into the dark room as she called his name softly.

"Alex?" She moved a couple of feet into the room. "Alex, where are you?"

"I'm right here, Duchess."

His voice came from right beside her and she jumped, startled by the sound. Reaching out, she felt his chest, then his face. When she knew for certain it was actually him, she drew back and punched him in the shoulder.

"You scared me," she accused. "Where were you anyway? I saw something move behind the couch."

"That was me." He moved her toward the door as they talked. "I was trying to keep from sneezing. Charles really should talk to his cleaning people. The dust was thick back there."

"I thought I'd die when I saw Alvarez sit on the couch." She paused. "Alex, it just occurred to me that they spoke English the whole time . . . except a French word now and then. Why would they do that?"

"I don't know," he said, shrugging. "Charles has always spoken English more than French because his business is based in Canada, and I believe Alvarez spent quite a bit of time in the States."

"It still seems strange. Almost as though they were speaking for our benefit."

"If they had known we were there, Duchess, we wouldn't be standing here wasting time," he said dryly. "We would be in the middle of a very nasty situation."

"Where are we going?" she asked as he cracked the door and peered around it into the hall.

"Guess?" he said, turning to give her an expectant look over his shoulder.

She thought for a moment. "Alvarez," she said finally. "We get to follow him to the cottage . . ." She paused thoughtfully. "Alex, you don't suppose this cottage is in Tibet or Siberia or Swaziland, do you?"

He chuckled and put his arm around her waist as they stepped out into the hall. "Why do you ask?"

"After all we've been through chasing this man, it just seemed a likely possibility." Suddenly she gasped. "Alex, look at you! You're all dirty."

They quickly dusted his clothing, then walked briskly through the entrance hall, nodding to the people who stared after the hastily retreating rumpled figures.

"They probably all think we were fooling around in the wine cellar," she said, her voice disgruntled as they once again followed the red Jaguar. They had had to run to the Renault in order to catch Alvarez as he left and were now right behind him as he took a winding country road in the general direction of Paris.

"Instead we were fooling around in the study." He chuckled quietly.

"We were not," she objected indignantly. "Any fooling around we did, we did in the bedroom."

She looked away from his wide grin and leaned back in the seat to stare at the taillights of the Jaguar in the distance. Alvarez certainly had kept them busy.

About thirty miles outside the city he turned into a narrow drive. Alex stopped the car immediately, turning off the lights as he stared thoughtfully into the heavily wooded area Alvarez had entered.

"There's no traffic down there. He'll notice our lights," he said, then shrugged in what Kate felt was a much too casual movement and turned into the drive also . . . only without headlights. "Let's just hope there's enough moonlight to keep us on the road."

It was eerie driving through the heavily wooded area in the dark. The night-blackened trees closed in around them, guarding the road with what she felt sure was brooding menace. Staring wide-eyed at their surroundings, Kate tried to pick out the road. She had never realized there were so many different shades of black.

They could see Alvarez's headlights shining through the trees ahead of them for perhaps fifteen minutes, then suddenly they were extinguished.

Alex immediately pulled the Renault off the drive into the trees. "We'll have to walk from here," he said, opening his door. "He'll be listening for the sound of Charles's car." He paused and glanced back at her. "And I'm afraid we'll have to keep off the road. It would be too easy for our friend Charles to take us by surprise."

Kate had held her peace when he had turned off the lights and driven blindly. She had even bitten her tongue to keep from protesting when he calmly said, "We'll walk," but this was too much.

"Alex," she whispered as he leaned down to open her door, "even though I'm wearing four-inch heels and an evening dress, I'll walk . . . but aren't there animals and bogs and things out there in those woods?"

His quiet chuckle drifted softly through the night. "We still have our flashlights, Duchess."

"Why, of course we do," she said sweetly, slapping her head with her hand at her stupidity. "So if we are attacked by crazed animals we can beat them off with our penlights." She stepped from the car, muttering, "Unless we run across a band of marauding chipmunks, we're sunk."

"Kate . . . Kate," he said, hugging her to him as she stepped from the car. She could feel his body shaking with laughter. "How did I get along before I met you?"

"You were a miserable playboy," she said, giving him a kiss on his rough cheek. It was a subject she wanted to explore more fully, but she knew there wasn't time. "You sat around with a redhead on each arm and cried in your champagne because there was no one to bitch at you."

"That's it," he said. "That's it exactly." Giving her one last hug, he glanced about quickly, his face alert. "Okay, Duchess, let's go."

He directed his light to the right of them. "The headlights on his car were coming from that direction when he killed them, so if we walk through here instead of walking beside the road, we'll probably get there quicker."

She only muttered a very little bit as they moved into brush that had to bear a decided resemblance to Darkest Africa. Because of the underbrush and fallen logs, they were forced to walk single file using their small flashlights to pick out a rough trail.

After a few minutes of walking Kate's feet were killing her. She had already tripped three times and she was out of breath, but she didn't say anything . . . at least not out loud. She knew she could have stayed in the car, but the knowledge didn't help her feet.

James Bond has warped the mind of the American male, she thought cynically as she tripped again.

Alex stopped and leaned against a tree, pulling her to him. "How are you doing, Katy?"

He wasn't even breathing hard, damn him. "I'm hunky-dory," she said mildly, struggling to slow down her breathing. "I've broken three nails and could possibly have a run in my leg rather than my stocking, but I'm fine."

He shifted, settling her between his legs. "You're terrific," he said, his lips moving against her forehead.

She nodded. "A lesser woman would have crumbled," she acknowledged modestly.

"A lesser woman would have taken a cab back to Monte Carlo, but then all women are lesser compared to you." He chuckled, then nodded slowly to indicate something behind her. "We're almost there."

She raised her head and glanced in that direction. She couldn't make out the house, but she could see light that must have been coming from its windows.

"What are we going to do when we get there?" she asked, letting her head sink back to his comfortable chest.

"We wait."

"As long as we're sitting I guess that won't be so bad," she murmured.

As far as Kate was concerned, they could have stayed just exactly as they were, with his strong arms around her and their bodies pressed together. However, they began walking again as soon as she caught her breath and before long they could see, in the center of a small clearing, a stone cottage, its walls heavy with vines.

Moving to the side of the cottage, they found a fallen log a safe distance away and sat down to wait. Since talking was risky, Kate leaned against Alex and listened to the sounds of the night. She could have been back in Plum, rather than a few miles outside of Paris. The sounds animals made in the night were universal.

The bark of the log penetrated her jersey dress, but it wasn't unpleasant. Someday perhaps she would take Alex to her cabin in the rough country of West Texas and sit with him like this beside a campfire. She longed to show him the Texas stars, stars bigger and brighter and friendlier than anywhere else in the world.

For a long time she was lost in pleasant dreams, then suddenly she felt Alex's head jerk up. She listened closely and after a few seconds heard the distinct hum of an approaching car.

Alex slid with her to the grass behind the log, and as they watched from the woods a large dark car appeared around the bend in the road. Seconds later its headlights were extinguished and Sauset stepped out.

As soon as he entered the cottage, Alex stood and stealthily began to move closer in a crouching walk. Kate was right behind him, as close as his shadow, her heart pounding as they stopped beside a lighted window. They bent down, staying close to the wall, and waited.

"I've decided what the next move is to be."

Sauset's voice was muffled, but his words were clear to the two hidden outside the window. "It's time to show Blakewell that I'm serious."

"And how do you plan to accomplish that?" Alvarez sounded faintly amused, as though he were participating in some kind of a game instead of tampering with people's lives.

"Don't you mean, how will *you* accomplish that?"

"Very well, how will I?"

"You're going to England . . . tonight," Sauset stated. He talked slowly, but there was a hectic quality about his voice. "You'll tell him that unless he gives up his plans to go to America immediately, you'll inform the newspapers and his wife of the, shall we say, mistake in his past . . . then give him the letter."

"That sounds interesting," Alvarez said. "But not tonight. I've already canceled too many plans for this crazy scheme of yours. This time it will have to be at my pleasure."

So the worm is going to turn, Kate thought, shooting Alex a look of surprise. At the château Alvarez had seemed to be nothing more than a hired hand. Now, as though he had done some powerful thinking on the way to the cottage and had arrived at some interesting conclusions, the Parisian was assuming the upper hand.

Sauset must have recognized the change also for when he spoke again he sounded angry and not a little weary. "Aren't you forgetting about the money that I keep depositing in your account?" Sauset countered. "Don't tell me you're going to do without it?"

"But I won't have to." Alvarez laughed. "Who will you get to deliver your nice little letters if you let me go? Would you like to take them yourself, Charles?"

Kate didn't recognize the words Sauset used next and she was glad. Eventually he calmed down, but his voice was unsteady as he said, "Very well. When can you go?"

Kate almost felt sorry for him. Alvarez seemed to be taking quite a bit of pleasure in holding him under his thumb. Her suspicion was confirmed when the Parisian spoke again.

"I'll have to get back to you on that, Charles," he said smoothly. "You won't have to wait for more than a week or so."

There was no sound from the room for a few seconds, then they heard classical music. Another minute ticked by before Sauset said, "Well, what are you waiting for? You've tormented me just as you intended. Why don't you leave me in peace?" Then the music grew louder and any reply Alvarez had intended to make was lost.

As soon as Alvarez walked out, Alex motioned for Kate to stay and crept around the corner of the cottage. She did as he wanted and waited . . . for a few seconds. Biting her lip anxiously she listened to the violent sounds of Wagner coming from inside, then she couldn't stand the tension any longer and moved silently to follow him.

Peering around the corner of the cottage, she saw Alvarez walking toward his car. When he extended his hand toward the door, Alex stepped out from behind Sauset's car and Kate held her breath.

"Going somewhere, René?" Alex asked casually.

Alvarez swung around and Kate prepared herself for an unpleasant argument. But something went wrong. Instead of the verbal confrontation she had expected, Alvarez spat out an angry epithet, then rushed at Alex.

For one frozen moment, the figures of the struggling men were silhouetted against the moonlit sky, then they fell awkwardly to the ground and Kate couldn't distinguish one from the other. She ran forward, pulling her dress above her knees as she went because it persisted in becoming entangled in her evening sandals.

When she reached them, Alex appeared to have the upper hand. He was sprawled on top of Alvarez, his hands holding his shoulders down. Then somehow the Parisian managed to get his forearm against Alex's throat and was forcing his head back at a painful-looking angle.

Kate stood watching helplessly, then sucked in her breath harshly when she saw Alvarez reach into his jacket with his free hand and pull out a gun.

"Alex," she called out. "He's got a gun."

Alex lashed out viciously to strike his opponent's hand and the gun went flying. It spun through the air and hit the ground a few feet away, then slithered out of sight beneath the low-slung Jaguar.

Glancing back anxiously, she found to her dismay that the advantage Alex had gained was only momentary. Seconds later the Frenchman surprised him by clasping his hands together tightly and slamming them sideways into the vulnerable area of Alex's throat.

Kate heard the blow connect with sickening force and knew Alex was stunned by the pain. Alvarez used the moment to grab him by the hair and slam his head into the bumper of Sauset's car. The first blow made Kate dizzy and she pressed her hands to her mouth as his head met the bumper again and again.

She stopped a scream of agony from erupting when she suddenly remembered the gun. Rushing forward, she fell to her knees beside the sports car. She began to run her hand frantically over the ground in the area she felt it must be, but her fingers met nothing other than rough stone. She muttered a violent curse, then, lying flat on the ground, she reached beneath the car, praying feverishly that she would find it. Then as she moved her hand to the left again, her fingers grazed something metallic and cold.

She could feel the crushed rock pressing into her breasts and her thighs as she wedged herself even farther under the car, but she simply couldn't grasp it. Even when she felt it was hopeless, the painful sounds of the struggle taking place just a few feet away spurred her on.

With two fingers she pulled steadily at the barrel of the gun. She had managed to move it a quarter of an inch when it slipped from between her perspiring fingers and the barrel moved out of reach.

Kate could have cried. For a second her head dropped forward in defeat, but only for a second. Stretching her arms to the limit, she moved her hand over the rough surface of the ground beneath the car, then she drew in a startled breath. When the barrel had slid away, the butt of the gun had moved closer, and she was able to pull it toward her, getting a firm grip on it at last.

She was on her knees with the gun extended before she realized that the fight was over and Alex was pulling the defeated Alvarez to his feet. Slumping against the car in relief, she carefully laid down the gun and allowed her hands to shake as much as they wanted to.

"Katy," Alex called, his voice quiet but intense. "Are you all right?"

"I'm fine," she said weakly. "I found the gun." She gingerly picked it up again and stood up. She could feel her knees trying to fold beneath her, but wouldn't allow herself to collapse when she had come this far. Reaching Alex, she handed him the gun and, even though she had fought so hard to get it, she was very relieved to be rid of it again.

He grinned down at her and said, "Thanks, Duchess," as he put his arm around her to pull her against him. She caught a glimpse of his battered face before he turned back to where Alvarez leaned against Sauset's car. "Now, Alvarez, I think there was something you wanted to tell us."

The dark man glared at Alex, his breath coming in harsh gasps, but he didn't speak.

Now that she was standing close to Alex, and she knew he was all right, Kate felt herself relaxing. René Alvarez didn't scare her anymore. Nothing scared her as long as she was with Alex.

"I think you should tell him, René," she said in a confiding tone as she leaned toward him. "Sometimes Alex gets mean." She shook her head. "I tell him over and over that it's not nice to hurt people, but he will insist on doing strange things to their kneecaps."

"Shut up, bitch," Alvarez snarled.

Alex's head snapped up at the man's words. "Bitch?" he said, his voice low and deadly, then he raised an eyebrow in inquiry as he repeated "Bitch?" and he grabbed Alvarez by the throat to shove him back against the car.

"Alex." She sighed. "You don't have to defend my honor. It's just not necessary."

He stared down at her. "It's necessary for me, Katy," he said softly.

Kate couldn't even pull up a short reply as she met the loving look in his midnight eyes. She simply gazed at him as her insides melted.

"Your halo is slipping," he murmured, reaching out to touch her hair. "There's nothing more intriguing than an angel with a crooked halo."

She swayed toward him, then choking sounds began to penetrate the magic he had woven. "Alex," she said. "Do you hear funny noises?"

They reluctantly turned back to Alvarez to find his eyes wide and his face turning purple. As Alex released him, he inhaled in a harsh gust.

"Now," Alex said in annoyance. "Tell me what Sauset is using to blackmail Tony."

"I don't—" He broke off abruptly as Alex took a step forward. "Letters!" he said hastily. "There are some letters. Charles doesn't tell me anything, but he occasionally takes the letters out. Afterward he always gets very drunk."

Alex was silent for a moment, then he turned to Kate. "I don't want him to leave until I talk to Charles, Duchess . . . that is, if Charles didn't leave by the back door when he heard all the racket."

"I don't think he heard, Alex." She glanced back to the cottage. "He has Wagner turned up to a deafening level." She hesitated, then drew in a breath and said, "What do you want me to do?"

He squeezed her waist. "That's my girl. Do you think you can hold the gun on him for a while?"

Kate felt her heart leap in her breast, but she said, "Are you kidding? Of course I can."

She swallowed noisily, wiped her hands on her dress, then reached out for the gun. He gave it to her, watching her closely, and for a moment she felt her hand shaking. Then inhaling deeply, she blew the hair out of her eyes before turning to face Alvarez.

"Okay," she said firmly, motioning with the gun. "Back up against the car."

When he merely stared at her insolently, she narrowed her eyes and twisted her lips in what she hoped was a nasty smile. "Go ahead. Make my day."

Alex smothered a whoop of startled laughter. "God, Katy. I do love you," he said, then without another word he turned to walk back to the cottage.

Lord, what a time to tell me something like that, she thought as she fought to keep her eyes on Alvarez instead of Alex's retreating back. Now that her breathing had returned to its normal rate, she could hear the music coming from behind her, and in the seconds after he entered the cottage it seemed to take on ominous tones.

She strained her ears as the minutes ticked away and once she thought she heard shouting over the music, but she couldn't be sure. Then suddenly the stereo was switched off and silence filled the night.

She could hear Alvarez breathing and the sound grated on her nerves. As perspiration formed on her forehead, she was grateful for the darkness that hid her anxious face. There was nothing she could do except stay where she was and keep the gun on Alvarez.

But the gun was growing unreasonably heavy and her hand began to shake with the effort she was making to keep it pointed in the right direction.

Suddenly she caught her breath sharply as a new sound penetrated the stillness, the sound of footsteps on the crushed-rock drive. She waited silently, keeping her gaze steadily on the man in front of her. Then when she felt her arm sag slightly, she caught movement from the corner of her eye and a second later Alex was there beside her.

Ten

"Alex," she said, and he could hear the relief in her voice as he drew closer. "You were gone so long, you had me worried."

"I'm fine," he said as she gratefully returned the gun. Pocketing the weapon, he turned to Alvarez. "You can go now, but listen to me—if you so much as look in Tony Blakewell's direction again, I'll find you. And then you'll pay very strict attention to me, I assure you."

They watched him drive away, then Alex pulled her into his arms and buried his face in her throat. He had never spent a longer ten minutes in his life than when he knew she was alone with Alvarez. It hadn't made his temper any sweeter when he had dealt with Charles. He only hoped that she understood why he had had to do it.

It was a while before he could speak, but when her warmth began to still the quakes that shook his insides, he drew back.

"Kate—" His voice was raspy and he inhaled to begin again. "Kate, if I ever get you into anything like this again you have my permission to kick my butt."

"I'll remember that," she said, laughing shakily. She reached up to touch his face. "What about Sauset? What happened in there? What did he tell you?"

With his arm around her, he began walking reluctantly toward the cottage. "He hasn't told me anything yet," he told her. "He merely agreed—reluctantly—that he would."

When they walked into the living room of the small cottage, Sauset was sitting stiffly upright in a wooden chair, a silk handkerchief held to his lip.

"All right, Charles," Alex said wearily. "Let's hear it. How did you find out about Hélène and her abortion? And why are you hounding Tony?"

"I *loved* her!" he spat out. "And she loved me. She would have been mine if he hadn't killed her."

"Tony didn't kill Hélène," Alex said quietly, then after a moment he continued. "Charles, I didn't know that you were involved with Hélène. Were you seeing her at the same time Tony was?"

Sauset stared at him for a moment as though he were unwilling to talk, then he smiled. "Yes, I was. And that pleased me. At least . . . at least it did at first. I enjoyed knowing that he thought he had her exclusively all the time she was sleeping with me. That made me feel good. It made . . ." His voice trailed away, then in a moment he inhaled and said stiffly, "Then later I wanted her all to myself, but she wasn't built that way. At least I had the consolation of knowing she wouldn't stay with Blakewell either. She could never be satisfied with only one man."

"She doesn't sound like a very nice person," Alex suggested cautiously.

"Nice?" He laughed. "That sounds like the kind of coddled-egg word you would use, Alex." He stared at him. "I never minded you so much. You were always a little simpleminded, but still you had to struggle just like everyone else. You didn't have the golden touch like—" He stopped abruptly and glanced away as he pressed the handkerchief to his mouth again.

"Like Tony?" he asked, but Sauset merely stared at the floor. After a moment Alex tried again. "I can understand why you dislike Tony. You both loved the same woman; wars have been started over less than that, but why wait all these years to start harassing him?"

"Wait?" Sauset jerked his head up and began to laugh. "What makes you think I've waited?"

"What are you talking about?" Alex stared at him in bewilderment, then shook his head. Sauset looked as though he had finally gone over the edge. His eyes showed it and so did his slurred speech, but Alex couldn't let that stop him. He had to put an end to this now. "Are you saying this is not the first time you've tried to blackmail Tony?"

"Blackmail? Yes, I guess you could call it that," he said. "I'll admit it doesn't have the panache that my other schemes have had, but I was pressed."

He shrugged, then after a moment he looked Alex in the eye. "Do you remember what Tony was worth in college? A fortune," he said without waiting for Alex to answer. "He had everything he wanted. Not only money, but everything. It was all handed to him. I watched it happening and I hated him. Why should it all fall into his lap? The man was *stupid*, for God's sake. Everyone knew that without his friends' help, he wouldn't have made it through school at all."

His lips twitched into an ugly facsimile of a smile. "But his good luck didn't last, did it?" He glanced up at Alex. "What do you think happened to all his money?"

Alex's eyes narrowed, then he said slowly, "Tony said his father made a series of bad investments just shortly before he died."

"He said, he said," Sauset mimicked. "He didn't *know*. He didn't know the stock I had to buy, the businesses I let go bankrupt. It was pure genius." He laughed again and the sound wasn't pleasant. "Do you know how many acting parts your precious Tony has lost because of me? Dozens. And do you remember the time he was injured in a hit-and-run accident?" He pounded his chest with his fist. "It was *me*. All me."

Sauset stood up unsteadily. "All these years I've watched things fall apart for him . . . and I was content." He held his head cocked to the side as though he couldn't figure out what went wrong.

Suddenly Sauset shook his head sharply and looked around. After a moment, he extended his hand to Alex in the weirdest switch Kate had ever seen.

"I'll have to be going now, Alex," he said quietly, shaking his hand. "It was interesting seeing you again." With that he walked out the door of the cottage.

For a moment Kate was stunned, then when she heard a motor start up she moved to follow him, but Alex caught her arm. "Alex?" she asked in bewilderment as the strange man began to drive away.

"Let him go, Kate," he said, his voice sounding strangely weary. He stooped down to pick up the letters Sauset had dropped.

Kate paced restlessly as he sat down and scanned each one, then let them fall back to the floor. "Come on, Duchess," he said, reaching for her. "Let's go home."

But they didn't go home or even back to Monte Carlo. They were both too exhausted and too sore to make it any farther than Pete's apartment outside Paris.

It was quite a while later when Kate raised her head from where it rested on a floating cushion in the bathtub and watched Alex come into the room and stoop beside her.

"I wondered if you were going to sleep in here," he said, smiling down at her. He had already bathed and was dressed in the clothes he had bought earlier in the day—a cream knit shirt and black slacks.

"I haven't been in here that long," she protested.

Reaching down, he grabbed one of her feet and pulled it above the thick layer of bubbles. "You see," he said. "Pruny toes."

"I don't care," she said. "I'm not coming out yet. I'm just now beginning to feel human again."

He stared down at her for a moment, then shrugged. "Well, if you won't come out"—he slipped off his shoes and swung his legs around into the water—"I guess I'll just have to come in."

"Alex!" she gasped, laughing as the bubbles covered his fully clothed body.

He reached out and pulled her forward until she lay full-length against him, then ran his hands down her body, his spread fingers resting on her slippery buttocks.

"I knew there was something I liked about this bathtub," she murmured.

With his chin resting on his chest he grinned down at her. "Somehow I feel a little overdressed."

"My very thought," she murmured as she helped him peel off his shirt. She watched thoughtfully, with her elbows propped on the wooden deck, as he stripped off the soggy slacks.

When he was back in the water and they were sitting together at the end of the tub, she reached up to touch his bruised face. "Alex," she said softly. "Why did you let him go? After all the damage he's done Tony?"

He let out a harsh gust of air. "He didn't do all those things, Kate. In fact, I doubt if he was responsible for any of the things he talked about."

"You mean he made it all up?" she asked incredulously.

"No, I think he really believes he's responsible," he said, his voice sad. "I think he's a very sick man."

"But can you be sure?"

"As soon as he mentioned Tony's accident, I was positive. The man who ran Tony down was a drunk. They caught him six months after the accident." He stroked her wet body unconsciously as he talked. "Then I started thinking about Tony's father and his investments. I checked those out, Kate, as soon as I found out that Tony had inherited virtually nothing. There's just no way Charles could have done the things he claims he did. Tony's father was foolish and in some instances criminally negligent, but there was no intrigue involved . . . no bankrupt businesses."

He laughed shortly. "There wasn't even any of

that 'evidence' that he talked about in his blackmail letters. Those letters from Hélène contained nothing about that."

She was silent for a moment as she took in what he was saying. "What will he do now?" she asked finally. "Won't he continue harassing Tony?"

He shrugged. "After I explain to Tony, it won't make any difference." He paused. "You know, I remembered something about Charles that I had forgotten when I was telling you about the whole thing, and I think it may be where this all began. Once, just before he met Hélène, Tony told me he had caught Charles cheating on an exam. Tony didn't think much about it—you remember we already knew Charles was a little peculiar—but he said he felt sorry for him. The odd thing was that apparently Tony let Charles see that he pitied him. He said Charles had a look in his eyes like he'd never seen before."

He paused, shifting to pull her closer in an unconscious gesture. "I remember he laughed when he told me about it, but I could tell it bothered him. He said he thought that at that moment, Charles wanted to kill him."

"You think Charles hated Tony because he pitied him?"

"I think it had to be something like that. I know I wouldn't react very well to pity and I'm relatively sane." She nodded slowly, seeing his point. "It was after that that Charles stopped hanging around us. The malignancy must have been growing already. Over the years he kept an eye on Tony, and as long as he was struggling to get along like the rest of us, Charles was fine. Because he wished disasters on Tony and because his mind was weak, he began to think he had made them happen. He must have read about the movie contract and decided to do something more substantial."

She shivered. "Shouldn't he be in a hospital, getting some kind of help?"

"He could get help if he wanted it," he said solemnly. "But he's done no one any physical harm except in his mind. There's not much we could do other than inform the police . . . and I don't think even Tony would want to do that."

She sat silently rubbing Alex's soapy chest for a moment, then said slowly, "Alex, were all those letters from Hélène?"

He nodded without speaking.

"Do you . . . do you think she really loved him like he said?" She didn't know why she wanted to know. Perhaps because it would end the sad story.

"I don't know, Kate," he said softly. "But he believes she did and I guess that's important to him."

He pulled her tightly to him as though he, too, were affected by the ending of the sad, old love story. Kate held his head to her breasts, touching his hair with gentle strokes. The past was over. That story was finished. It was time for them to get on with their own story.

"You know what I love about you?" she murmured.

He raised his head quickly, and as he did, his midnight eyes began to sparkle with amusement. "Do you love something about me?" he asked.

"I love a lot of things about you . . . but we'll talk about that later," she added hastily when the sparkle in his eyes grew to a full-fledged flame. "I love the way you treat me like an equal. As though I count. There's never any of that 'little lady' stuff with you."

"You're trying to tell me I haven't been opening the doors for you or pulling out your chairs?"

"You know I don't mean that," she said,
laughing. "I'm delighted because you don't leave
me out of your life and your decisions . . . even the
big ones. You treat me as though I have a brain
and know how to use it. You let me come along
with you on a mission that was very important to
you."

"You mean, I almost got you killed," he said
gruffly.

"No one almost got killed. And we had no way
of knowing Alvarez was carrying a gun." She stared
at him stubbornly. "And even if we had known, I
would still have gone with you. You handle yourself real well for a Yankee," she added.

"I'm afraid I didn't do a very good job of pro-
tecting you tonight," he said dryly. He touched
the bruise on her shoulder, then bent down to kiss
it.

"You were dynamite," she insisted. "You got
the better of Alvarez even after we had walked all
that way through the jungle."

"The 'jungle' was only half a mile wide, Duchess," he said. "And I beat Alvarez only because I
used strategy."

"What kind of strategy?" she asked curiously.

"Oh, it's a trick I learned years ago," he said
casually. "You simply let them beat you senseless
to tire them out, then you take them."

She chuckled. "You can stop putting yourself
down," she told him. "Besides, your massive forearms aren't your only attraction. You have other
redeeming traits." She paused, regarding him
solemnly. "Alex, I know that you didn't have to
leave me with Alvarez. There were a dozen other
things you could have done with him, but you

didn't. You let me watch him because you knew it was important to me."

She pulled down his head to kiss him. "Thanks for doing it. It made me feel like an equal . . . no, even more—I felt like Charlemagne's daughter."

"I didn't know he had a daughter. What did she do?"

"She carried her lover to her bedroom on her back so that there would be only one set of footprints showing in the snow." She sighed. "They don't make women like that anymore."

"Thank God," he said vehemently. "She was probably built like a water buffalo. I think I'm glad they don't make them like that anymore."

"I'd do it," she insisted. "I'd carry you on my back—that is, if I could lift you, I would."

"That's my point," he said, sliding down to kiss her breasts, then up to kiss her nose. "You are definitely not built like a water buffalo."

Pulling her knee up across his thigh, she unconsciously began to move it back and forth over his wet body. "I'm glad if you're glad," she said, then she fell silent, her brow creasing in thought. After a moment she said, "You know, cartooning is going to seem awfully dull after all this. It's going to take me a while to settle down again."

Alex didn't speak right away. He reached down to run a hand over her derrière and thigh, pressing her closer, then he sighed. "Do you have to settle down again, Katy?" At her puzzled look, he continued. "I guess what I'm trying to say is—" He suddenly stood up, dumping her with a splash that showered her confused face.

"You're trying to say what?" she demanded as she climbed from the tub.

"I'm trying to say that now we're both pruny,"

he said, his voice muffled by the towel as he dried off and walked into the bedroom at the same time.

"No you weren't," she said hotly, following him from the bathroom. "That wasn't what you were going to say at all. What on earth is wrong with you? You haven't been shy about telling me anything since we met." She snorted. "Shy! Lord, that's a laugh. You've bulldozed me from the first moment you saw me. You've—"

She stopped speaking abruptly when he swung around to face her. He stared down at her for a moment, then sighed and pulled her onto the bed. Reaching up, he pulled the hairpins from her hair and let it fall into his hands.

"Alex?" she prompted in bewilderment.

He looked up from her hair. "I simply wanted to ask you if you had ever thought about . . . about visiting Wisconsin," he said gruffly.

"Visiting?" she asked, turning around to stare at him.

"All right! Have you ever thought of living there?" He slumped slightly as though it were a great relief simply to have said it.

She sucked in a sharp breath. "In Wisconsin?" she whispered, then swallowed in agitation. "I've . . . I've always wanted to see Wisconsin."

"Kate," he said, framing her face to stare down at her. "I'm asking you to marry me."

"Yes—yes, I know," she replied, her voice distracted. "I'm thinking."

"About what, for God's sake!" he said shortly.

She slowly lifted her gaze to stare into his eyes. "Alex, we've known each other for three days."

He looked stunned for a moment, then said, "Well, okay. So we've known each other for three days."

Before she could say anything else he stood

and walked a few feet away, then turned back abruptly. "I know what you're doing. You're giving me that 'normal' business again. I thought you promised not to do that."

"And I thought you promised not to push me," she said irritably.

"So who's pushing?" he said, shrugging casually, but avoiding her eyes. After a moment, he said, "Okay. I'm pushing. But tell me this—if we had known each other for three months or three years, what would your answer be then?"

She bit her lip, then sighed and answered honestly. "I guess I'd say there's nowhere on earth I'd rather be than Wisconsin if you're there."

He exhaled explosively and pulled her to him. "Then I can wait," he said, kissing her fiercely. A hard, hungry kiss that ended only when he pulled back and grinned at her. "At least, I can wait to get married. There are some things that I can't wait for."

"Gimme a for instance," she murmured, leaning her chin on his chest to look up at him cockily.

"How about"—he spoke lazily as he led her toward the bed—"how about I show you a for instance," he finished as they fell onto the bed with their arms entwined.

And so, like the practical, sane people they were, they waited to get married . . . they waited for as long as it took to fly back to Wisconsin and obtain a marriage license.

Six months later, Kate and Alex walked down a street in Madison. Spring was finally beginning to take hold and the air was as sparkling clear as fine champagne.

Kate hadn't managed to bring about her world-shaking cartoon soap. Instead she had created what she considered her masterpiece. It was an adventure cartoon using a husband-and-wife team as the main characters. At last she was able to use *Splak!* and *Kapow!* as often as she wanted to.

The cartoon had been so successful, Kate had been approached recently about a Saturday-morning television series. It was an offer she was still considering as she and Alex walked toward the restaurant where they had reservations for lunch.

"So . . . what do you think?" she asked again.

"I think you'll figure it out by yourself without my interference," Alex said, laughing at her disgruntled features.

"What's a husband for if not to interfere?" she muttered. "I know *I'd* interfere if it were your business."

"And have done so many times in the past," he added cheerfully.

"Exactly," she said. "And it's the very least you can do for me."

"So sign the contract," he said finally.

"But—"

"So don't sign it," he said, interrupting her. Pulling to a stop, he pushed her against the wall of a building and bent to give her a slow, heart-stopping kiss. When he pulled away, he said softly, "Kate, I'd love to help you out on this, but you're the only one who can say if it's what you want to do. Now do you understand?"

For a few seconds her hand remained on the top of her head, holding onto her wide-brimmed hat, and her eyes remained closed. When she opened them at last to look up at him, they were dreamy and docile.

"Yes," she whispered, then cleared her throat. "Yes, I understand."

They had walked several feet when she suddenly stopped walking and stared up at him. "You did it again!" she accused. "Why do you do that every time we have an argument?"

"I thought you liked it," he said, his look guileless.

"Well . . . that's not the point. It always puts me off so I forget what I was saying."

"Uh-huh," he said agreeably.

"It's not fair, dammit," she said, but she grinned as she said it because he was irresistible and he knew it.

They began walking again and she turned the problem of the series over in her mind. It would take up so much of her time, time she wanted to give to Alex instead. Later they would start a family and that would take some of the intimate moments away from them, moments they had come to treasure in their almost six months of marriage. They should spend every minute with each other while they still could.

She turned to him to give him her decision when something odd caught her eye.

"Alex," she whispered. "Did you see that?"

"What?" he asked, glancing around.

Her forehead was creased with her intense concentration. "Those men." She nodded at the other side of the street. "You know, I saw something just like that on television the other night. Two men had packages that were wrapped exactly alike. When they bumped into each other, the packages dropped. Then they each picked up the other's package."

"Interesting," he said, staring down at her in curiosity.

"That's not all," she said urgently. "The men were dealing in drugs and one of the packages contained heroin; the other contained money."

"This is all very interesting, Duchess, but why are you telling me now?"

"Because those men"—she nodded sharply toward the street—"did the same thing." When he started to protest, she continued. "I swear it, Alex. They switched packages." She jerked her head around. "One of them is crossing the street," she hissed, then moved away from him to see around a couple who were walking toward them on the sidewalk.

"No, Kate," he said firmly as she looked back to grin at him, then began to follow the man. "Kate. Will you listen? Katy . . ."

THE EDITOR'S CORNER

Last month I told you about the long novels coming from LOVESWEPT authors in the Bantam Books' general list. And now this month you get a special treat: an excerpt from Sandra Brown's riveting historical romance, **SUNSET EMBRACE**. It's right in the back of this book and I'm sure the brief glimpse into the lives of Lydia and Ross will intrigue you so much that you'll want to ask your bookseller to hold a copy of **SUNSET EMBRACE** for you. It's due on the racks early next month.

Sandra really packs a double whammy for romance readers next month because you can also look forward to a LOVESWEPT from her! And "double whammy" is not only apt for the long historical plus short contemporary publication, but as a description of her LOVESWEPT #79. In **THURSDAY'S CHILD** heroine Allison is a twin. And she is persuaded to "pull a switch" by her sister Ann who couldn't be more different from Allison if she'd been born to other parents. And then along comes Spencer Raft—one of those extraordinarily dashing and sensual men that Sandra dreams up—and scientist Allison is the beneficiary of some very special "experimental" help from Spencer. **THURSDAY'S CHILD** is so humorous and has such wonderful love scenes that you definitely will *not* want to miss it!

With only two romances published (**BREAKING ALL THE RULES**, LOVESWEPT #61 and **CHARADE**, LOVESWEPT #74), Joan Elliott Pickart has certainly found her place in readers' hearts. Joan and all of us

(continued)

here are very grateful for your letters praising those books. Well, here's cause for rejoicing about her romances again: **THE FINISHING TOUCH,** LOVESWEPT #80. Paige Cunningham is one of the most heartwarming of heroines. I was routing for her from first word until last as she and Kellen Davis fell in love and confronted their problems. Paige is an interior decorator and Kellen is an actor. She is working on his new home and there are some truly comic scenes as Kellen traipses along to help her shop for furnishings. And there is a love scene of such compassion and tenderness between them that I am positive you will never forget **THE FINISHING TOUCH.**

I found Joan Bramsch's offering for next month— **THE LIGHT SIDE,** LOVESWEPT #81—a marvelous romance . . . spritely, downright funny and terribly touching. Savvy Alexander entertains at children's parties dressed as a clown. Balloons are her "signature," and when she meets hero Sky Brady she's in an elevator (stuck!) that's crammed with balloons. Sky comes to the rescue, but very soon decides he needs rescuing—emotionally—from one dynamite little lady clown. But there are major obstacles to overcome before these two wonderful folks can find true, committed love. **THE LIGHT SIDE** has its serious side too and will appeal to all your emotions.

Last—but never, never least—Iris Johansen is back! Iris interrupted work on her second long novel for Bantam to write two LOVESWEPTS. First, you'll delight in **WHITE SATIN,** LOVESWEPT #82, in which Iris portrays the trials and tribulations of Dany Alexander. Dany is reaching to win the gold in Olympic ice skating competition while trying desperately to achieve happiness with her mentor Anthony Malik. This is a love story in typical "Iris Johansen tradition"—glowingly emotional, fast-paced, and as deliciously sensual as that title, **WHITE SATIN.** Now, you know our lovably tricky Iris, so you'd better read carefully if you want to discover which of the secondary characters in **WHITE SATIN** will be the hero of her LOVESWEPT #86, coming month after next, **BLUE VELVET.**

May your New Year be filled with all the best things in life—the company of good friends and family, peace and prosperity, and, of course, love.

Warm wishes for a wonderful 1985 from all of us at LOVESWEPT,

Carolyn Nichols

Carolyn Nichols
   Editor
LOVESWEPT
Bantam Books, Inc.
666 Fifth Avenue
New York, NY 10103

Read this special preview of

Sunset Embrace

by Sandra Brown

Coming from Bantam Books this January

They were two untamed outcasts on a Texas-bound wagon train, two passionate travelers, united by need, threatened by pasts they could not outrun. . . .

Lydia Russell—voluptuous and russet-haired, fleeing from a secret shame, vowing that never again would a man, any man, overpower her. . . .

Ross Coleman—dark, brooding, and iron-willed, with the shadow of a lawless past in his piercing eyes, sworn to resist the temptation of his wanton longings. . . .

Fate threw them together on the same wild road, where they fought the breathtaking desire blazing between them, while the shadows of their enemies grew longer. As the wagon train rolled west, the danger of them drew ever closer, until a showdown with their pursuers was inevitable. Before it was over, Lydia and Ross would face death . . . the truth about each other . . . and the astonishing strength of their love. . . .

She liked the way his hair fell over his forehead. His head was bent over as he cleaned his guns. The rifle, already oiled and gleaming, was propped against the side of the wagon. Now he was working on a pistol. Lydia knew nothing of guns, but this particular one frightened her. Its steel barrel was long and slender, cold and lethal. Ross brought it up near his face and peered down the barrel, blowing on it gently. Then he concentrated on rubbing it again with a soft cloth.

Their first day of marriage had passed uneventfully. The weather was still gloomy, but it wasn't raining as steadily or as hard as it had been. Nevertheless, it was damp and cool and Lydia had spent most of the day in the wagon. Ross had gotten up early, while it was still dark, and had shuffled through trunks and boxes. He seemed intent on the task, and she had pretended to sleep, not daring to ask what he was doing. When she did get up and began to move about the wagon she noticed that everything that had belonged to Victoria was gone. She didn't know what Ross had done with Victoria's things, but there was nothing of hers left in the wagon.

Lydia watched him now as he unconsciously pushed back his hair with raking fingers. His hair was always clean and glossy, even when his hat had mashed it down. It was getting long over his neck and ears. Lydia thought the black strands might feel very good against her fingers if she ever had occasion to touch them, which she couldn't imagine having the nerve to do even if he would allow it. She doubted he would. He treated her politely, but never commenced a conversation, and certainly never touched her.

"Tell me about your place in Texas," she said softly, bringing his green eyes away from the pistol to meet hers in the glow of the single lantern. She was holding the baby, rocking him gently, although he had finished nursing for the night and was already sleeping. They were killing the minutes until it was time to go to bed.

"I don't know much about it yet," he said, turning his attention back to his project. He briefly told her the same story about John Sachs that he had told Bubba. "He sent for the deed and, when it came back in the mail, there was a surveyor's description attached to it."

His enthusiasm for the property overrode his restraint and the words poured out. "It sounds beautiful. Rolling pastureland. Plenty of water. There's a branch of the Sabine River that flows through a part of it. The report said it has two wooded areas with oak, elm, pecan, cottonwoods near the river, pine, dogwood—"

"I love dogwood trees in the springtime when they bloom," Lydia chimed in excitedly.

Ross found himself smiling with her, until he realized he was doing it and quickly ducked his head again. "First thing I'll have to do is build a corral for the horses and a lean-to for us." The word had fallen naturally from his lips. Us. He glanced at her furtively, but she was stroking Lee's head and watched the dark baby hair fall back into its swirls after it was disturbed. Lee's head was pillowed on her breasts. For an instant Ross thought of his own head there, her touching his hair that way with that loving expression on her face.

He shifted uncomfortably on his stool. "Then, before winter, I'll have to build a cabin. It won't be fancy," he said with more force than necessary, like he was warning her not to expect anything special from him.

She looked at him with unspoken reproach. "It'll be fine, whatever it is."

He rubbed the gun barrel more aggressively. "Next spring I hope all the mares foal. That'll be my start. And who knows, maybe I can sell timber off the land to make some extra money, or put Lucky out to stud."

"I'm sure you'll make a success of it."

He wished she wouldn't be so damned optimistic. It was contagious. He could feel his heart accelerating over the unlimited prospects of a place of his own with heavy woods and fertile soil, and a prize string of horses. And he wouldn't have to be looking over his shoulder all the time either. He had never been in Texas. There wouldn't be as much threat of someone recognizing him.

Lost in his memories, he snapped the barrel back into place, spun the loaded six-bullet chamber, and twirled the pistol on his index finger with uncanny talent before taking aim on an imaginary target.

Lydia stared at him with fascination. When it occurred to Ross what he had done out of reflex, he jerked his head around to see if she had noticed. Her dark amber eyes were wide with incredulity. He shoved the pistol into its holster as if to deny that it existed.

She licked her lips nervously. "How . . . how far is your land from Jefferson?"

"About a day's ride by wagon. Half a day on horseback. As near as I can figure it on the map."

"What will we do when we get to Jefferson?"

She had listened to the others in the train enough to know that Jefferson was the second largest city in Texas. It was an inland port in the northeastern corner of the state that was connected to the Red River via Cypress Creek and Caddo Lake. The Red flowed into the Mississippi in Louisiana. Jefferson was a commercial center with paddle-wheelers bringing supplies from the east and New Orleans in exchange for taking cotton down to the markets in that city. For settlers moving into the state, it was a stopping-off place where they purchased wagons and household goods before continuing their trek westward.

"We won't have any trouble selling the wagon. I hear there's a waiting list for them. Folks are camped for miles around just waiting for more wagons to be built. I'll buy a flatbed before we continue on."

Lydia had been listening, but her mind was elsewhere. "Would you like me to trim your hair?"

"What?" His head came up like a spring mechanism was operating it.

Lydia swallowed her caution. "Your hair. It keeps falling over your eyes. Would you like me to cut it for you?"

He didn't think that was a good idea. Damn. He *knew* that wasn't a good idea. Still, he couldn't leave the idea alone. "You've got your hands full," he mumbled, nodding toward Lee.

She laughed. "I'm spoiling him rotten. I should

have put him in his bed long ago." She turned to do just that, tucking the baby in a light blanket to keep the damp air off him.

She had on one of the shirtwaists and skirts he had financed the day before. He wasn't going to let it be said that Ross Coleman wouldn't take care of his wife, any more than he was going to let it be said that he was sleeping outside his own wagon when he had a new wife sleeping inside. It was hell on him and he didn't know how he was going to survive many more nights like the sleepless one he had spent last night. But his pride had to be served. After a suitable time when suspicions would no longer be aroused, he would start sleeping outside. Many of the men did, giving up the wagons to their wives and children.

She liked those new clothes. She had folded and refolded them about ten times throughout the day. Ross couldn't decide if she was a woman accustomed to having fine clothes who had fallen on bad times, or a woman who had never possessed any clothes so fine. When it came right down to it, he didn't know anything about her. But then, she didn't know about him either, nor did anyone else.

All he knew of her was that a man had touched her, kissed her, known her intimately. And the more Ross thought about that, the more it drove him crazy. Who was the man and where was he now? Every time Ross looked at her, he could imagine that man lying on her, kissing her mouth, her breasts, burying his hands in her hair, fitting his body deep into hers. What disturbed him most was that the image had begun to wear his face.

"Do you have any scissors?"

Ross nodded, knowing he was jumping from the frying pan into the fire and condemning himself to another night of sleepless misery. He wanted badly to hate her. He also wanted badly to bed her.

He resumed his seat on the stool after he had given her the scissors. She draped a towel around his neck and told him to hold it together with one hand. Then she stood away from him, tilting her head first to one side then the other as she studied him.

When she lifted the first lock of his hair, he caught her wrist with his free hand. "You aren't going to butcher me, are you? Do you know what you're doing?"

"Sure," she said, teasing laughter shining like a sunbeam in her eyes. "Who do you think cuts *my* hair?" His face drained of color and took on a sickly expression. She burst out laughing. "Scared you, didn't I?" She shook off his hand and made the first snip with the scissors. "I don't think you'll be too mutilated." She stepped behind him to work on the back side first.

His hair felt as good coiling over her fingers as she had thought it would. It was course and thick, yet silky. She played with it more than she actually cut, hoping to prolong the pleasure. They chatted inconsequentially about Lee, about the various members of the train, and laughed over Luke Langston's latest mischievous antic.

The dark strands fell to his shoulders and then drifted to the floor of the wagon as she deftly maneuvered the scissors around his head. It was an effort to keep his voice steady when her breasts pressed into his back as she leaned forward or glanced his arm as she moved from one spot to another. Once a clump of hair fell onto his ear. Lydia bent at the waist and blew on it gently. Ross's arm shot up and all but knocked her to the floor.

"What are you doing?" Her warm breath on his skin had sent shafts of desire firing through him like cannonballs. His hand all but made a garrote out of the towel around his neck. The other hand balled into a tight fist where it rested on the top of his thigh.

She was stunned. "I . . . I was . . . what? What did I do?"

"Nothing," he growled. "Just hurry the hell up and get done with this."

Her spirits sank. They had been having such an easy time. She had acutally begun to hope that he might come to like her. She moved around to his front, hoping to rectify whatever she had done to startle him so, but he had become even more still and tense.

Ross had decided that if she were to trim his hair, it was necessary for her fingers to be sliding through it. He had even decided that it was necessary for her to lay her hand along his cheek to turn his head. He had decided that this was going to feel good no matter how much he didn't want it to and that he might just as well sit back and enjoy her attention.

But when he had felt her breath, heavy and warm and fragrant, whispering around his ear, it had all the impact of a strike of lightning. The bolt went straight from his head to his loins and ignited them.

If that weren't bad enough, now she was standing in front of him between his knees—it had been only natural to open them so she could move closer and not have to reach so far. Her breasts were directly in his line of vision and looked as tempting as ripe peaches waiting to be picked. God, but didn't she know what she was doing? Couldn't she tell by the fine sheen of sweat on his face that she was driving him slowly crazy. Each time she moved, he was tantalized by her scent, by the supple grace of her limbs, by the rustling of the clothes against her body which hinted at mysteries worth discovering.

"I'm almost done," she said when he shifted restlessly on the stool. Her knees had come dangerously close to his vulnerable crotch.

Oh, God, no! She leaned down closer to trim the hair on the crown of his head. Raising her arms higher, her breasts were lifted as well. If he inclined forward a fraction of an inch, he would nuzzle her with his nose and chin and mouth, bury his face in the lushness and breathe her, imbibe her. His lips, with searching lovebites, would find her nipple.

He hated himself. He plowed through his memory, trying to recall a time when Victoria had been such a temptation to him, or a time when he had felt free to put his hands over her breasts for the sheer pleasure of holding them. He couldn't. Had there ever been such a time?

No. Victoria hadn't been the kind of woman who deliberately lured a man, reducing him to an animal. Every time Ross made love to Victoria it had been with reverence and an attitude of worship. He had entered her body as one walks into a church, a little ashamed for what he was, apologetic because he wasn't worthy, a supplicant for mercy, contrite that such a temple was defiled by his presence.

There was nothing spiritual in what he was feeling now. He was consumed by undiluted carnality. Lydia was a woman who inspired that in a man, who had probably inspired it as a profession, despite her denials. She was trying to work the tricks of her trade on him by looking and acting as innocent as a virgin bride.

Well, by God, it wasn't going to work!

"Your moustache needs trimming too."

"What?" he asked stupidly, by now totally disoriented. He saw nothing but the feminine form before him, heard nothing but the pounding of his own pulse.

"Your moustache. Be very still." Bending to the task, she carefully clipped away a few longish hairs in his moustache, working her mouth in the way she wanted his to go.

Had he been looking at her comical, mobile mouth, it might have made him laugh. Instead he had lowered his eyes to trace the arch of her throat. The skin of it looked creamy at the base before it melded into the more velvety texture of her chest that disappeared into the top of her shirtwaist. Did she smell more like honeysuckle or magnolia blossoms?

Every sensory receptor in his body went off like a fire bell when she lightly touched his moustache, brushing his lips free of the clipped hairs with her fingertips. First to one side, then the other, her finger glided over his mouth. The choice was his. He could either stop her, or he could explode.

He pushed her hands away and said gruffly, "That's enough."

"But there's one—"

"Dammit, I said that's enough," he shouted, whipping the towel from around his neck and flinging it to the floor as he came off the stool. "Clean this mess up."

Lydia was at first taken off guard by his rudeness and his curt order, but anger soon overcame astonishment. She grabbed his hand and slapped the scissors into his palm with a resounding whack. "You clean it up. It's your hair. And haven't you ever heard the words 'thank you' before?"

With that she spun away from him and, after having taken off her skirt and shirtwaist and carefully folding them, crawled into her pallet, giving him her back as she pulled the covers over her shoulders.

He stood watching her in speechless fury before turning away to find the broom.

#1 HEAVEN'S PRICE
By Sandra Brown
Blair Simpson had enclosed herself in the fortress of her dancing, but Sean Garrett was determined to love her anyway. In his arms she came to understand the emotions behind her dancing. But could she afford the high price of love?

#2 SURRENDER
By Helen Mittermeyer
Derry had been pirated from the church by her ex-husband, from under the nose of the man she was to marry. She remembered every detail that had driven them apart—and the passion that had drawn her to him. The unresolved problems between them grew . . . but their desire swept them toward surrender.

#3 THE JOINING STONE
By Noelle Berry McCue
Anger and desire warred within her, but Tara Burns was determined not to let Damon Mallory know her feelings. When he'd walked out of their marriage, she'd been hurt.

Damon had violated a sacred trust, yet her passion for him was as breathtaking as the Grand Canyon.

#4 SILVER MIRACLES
By Fayrene Preston
Silver-haired Chase Colfax stood in the Texas moonlight, then took Trinity Ann Warrenton into his arms. Overcome by her own needs, yet determined to have him on her own terms, she struggled to keep from losing herself in his passion.

#5 MATCHING WITS
By Carla Neggers
From the moment they met, Ryan Davis tried to outmaneuver Abigail Lawrence. She'd met her match in the Back Bay businessman. And Ryan knew the Boston lawyer was more woman than any he'd ever encountered. Only if they vanquished their need to best the other could their love triumph.

#6 A LOVE FOR ALL TIME
By Dorothy Garlock
A car crash had left its marks on Casey Farrow's beauty. So what were Dan

Murdock's motives for pursuing her? Guilt? Pity? Casey had to choose. She could live with doubt and fear . . . or learn a lesson in love.

#7 A TRYST WITH MR. LINCOLN?

By Billie Green
When Jiggs O'Malley awakened in a strange hotel room, all she saw were the laughing eyes of stranger Matt Brady . . . all she heard were his teasing taunts about their "night together" . . . and all she remembered was nothing! They evaded the passions that intoxicated them until . . . there was nowhere to flee but into each other's arms.

#8 TEMPTATION'S STING

By Helen Conrad
Taylor Winfield likened Rachel Davidson to a Conus shell, contradictory and impenetrable. Rachel battled for independence, torn by her need for Taylor's embraces and her impassioned desire to be her own woman. Could they both succumb to the temptation of the tropical paradise and still be true to their hearts?

#9 DECEMBER 32nd . . . AND ALWAYS

By Marie Michael
Blaise Hamilton made her feel like the most desirable woman on earth. Pat opened herself to emotions she thought she'd buried with her late husband. Together they were unbeatable as they worked to build the jet of her late husband's dreams. Time seemed to be running out and yet—would ALWAYS be long enough?

#10 HARD DRIVIN' MAN

By Nancy Carlson
Sabrina sensed Jacy in hot pursuit, as she maneuvered her truck around the racetrack, and recalled his arms clasping her to him. Was he only using her feelings so he could take over her trucking company? Their passion knew no limits as they raced full speed toward love.

#11 BELOVED INTRUDER

By Noelle Berry McCue
Shannon Douglas hated

Michael Brady from the moment he brought the breezes of life into her shadowy existence. Yet a specter of the past remained to torment her and threaten their future. Could he subdue the demons that haunted her, and carry her to true happiness?

#12 HUNTER'S PAYNE
By Joan J. Domning
P. Lee Payne strode into Karen Hunter's office demanding to know why she was stalking him. She was determined to interview the mysterious photographer. She uncovered his concealed emotions, but could the secrets their hearts confided protect their love, or would harsh daylight shatter their fragile alliance?

#13 TIGER LADY
By Joan J. Domning
Who *was* this mysterious lover she'd never seen who courted her on the office computer, and nicknamed her Tiger Lady? And could he compete with Larry Hart, who came to repair the computer and stayed to short-circuit her emotions? How could she choose between poetry and passion—between soul and Hart?

#14 STORMY VOWS
By Iris Johansen
Independent Brenna Sloan wasn't strong enough to reach out for the love she needed, and Michael Donovan knew only how to take—until he met Brenna. Only after a misunderstanding nearly destroyed their happiness, did they surrender to their fiery passion.

#15 BRIEF DELIGHT
By Helen Mittermeyer
Darius Chadwick felt his chest tighten with desire as Cygnet Melton glided into his life. But a prelude was all they knew before Cyg fled in despair, certain she had shattered the dream they had made together. Their hearts had collided in an instant; now could they seize the joy of enduring love?

#16 A VERY RELUCTANT KNIGHT
By Billie Green
A tornado brought them together in a storm cel-

lar. But Maggie Sims and Mark Wilding were anything but perfectly matched. Maggie wanted to prove he was wrong about her. She knew they didn't belong together, but when he caressed her, she was swept up in a passion that promised a lifetime of love.

#17 TEMPEST AT SEA
By Iris Johansen
Jane Smith sneaked aboard playboy-director Jake Dominic's yacht on a dare. The muscled arms that captured her were inescapable—and suddenly Jane found herself agreeing to a month-long cruise of the Caribbean. Jane had never given much thought to love, but under Jake's tutelage she discovered its magic . . . and its torment.

#18 AUTUMN FLAMES
By Sara Orwig
Lily Dunbar had ventured too far into the wilderness of Reece Wakefield's vast Chilean ranch; now an oncoming storm thrust her into his arms . . . and he refused to let her go. Could he lure her, step by seductive step, away from the life she had forged for herself, to find her real home in his arms?

#19 PFARR LAKE AFFAIR
By Joan J. Domning
Leslie Pfarr hadn't been back at her father's resort for an hour before she was pitched into the lake by Eric Nordstrom! The brash teenager who'd made her childhood a constant torment had grown into a handsome man. But when he began persuading her to fall in love, Leslie wondered if she was courting disaster.

#20 HEART ON A STRING
By Carla Neggers
One look at heart surgeon Paul Houghton Welling told JoAnna Radcliff he belonged in the stuffy society world she'd escaped for a cottage in Pigeon Cove. She firmly believed she'd never fit into his life, but he set out to show her she was wrong. She was the puppet master, but he knew how to keep her heart on a string.

#21 THE SEDUCTION OF JASON

By Fayrene Preston

On vacation in Martinique, Morgan Saunders found Jason Falco. When a misunderstanding drove him away, she had to win him back. Morgan acted as a seductress, to tempt him to return; she sent him tropical flowers to tantalize him; she wrote her love in letters twenty feet high—on a billboard that echoed the words in her heart.

#22 BREAKFAST IN BED

By Sandra Brown

For all Sloan Fairchild knew, Hollywood had moved to San Francisco when mystery writer Carter Madison stepped into her bed-and-breakfast inn. In his arms the forbidden longing that throbbed between them erupted. Sloan had to choose—between her love for him and her loyalty to a friend. . . .

#23 TAKING SAVANNAH

By Becky Combs

The Mercedes was headed straight for her! Cassie hurled a rock that smashed the antique car's taillight. The price driver Jake Kilrain exacted was a passionate kiss, and he set out to woo the Southern lady, Cassie, but discovered that his efforts to conquer the lady might end in his own surrender . . .

#24 THE RELUCTANT LARK

By Iris Johansen

Her haunting voice had earned Sheena Reardon fame as Ireland's mournful dove. Yet to Rand Challon the young singer was not just a lark but a woman whom he desired with all his heart. Rand knew he could teach her to spread her wings and fly free, but would her flight take her from him or into his arms forever?

LOVESWEPT

Love Stories you'll never forget by authors you'll always remember

☐	21603	**Heaven's Price** #1 Sandra Brown	$1.95
☐	21604	**Surrender** #2 Helen Mittermeyer	$1.95
☐	21600	**The Joining Stone** #3 Noelle Berry McCue	$1.95
☐	21601	**Silver Miracles** #4 Fayrene Preston	$1.95
☐	21605	**Matching Wits** #5 Carla Neggers	$1.95
☐	21606	**A Love for All Time** #6 Dorothy Garlock	$1.95
☐	21609	**Hard Drivin' Man** #10 Nancy Carlson	$1.95
☐	21610	**Beloved Intruder** #11 Noelle Berry McCue	$1.95
☐	21611	**Hunter's Payne** #12 Joan J. Domning	$1.95
☐	21618	**Tiger Lady** #13 Joan Domning	$1.95
☐	21613	**Stormy Vows** #14 Iris Johansen	$1.95
☐	21614	**Brief Delight** #15 Helen Mittermeyer	$1.95
☐	21616	**A Very Reluctant Knight** #16 Billie Green	$1.95
☐	21617	**Tempest at Sea** #17 Iris Johansen	$1.95
☐	21619	**Autumn Flames** #18 Sara Orwig	$1.95
☐	21620	**Pfarr Lake Affair** #19 Joan Domning	$1.95
☐	21321	**Heart on a String** #20 Carla Neggars	$1.95
☐	21622	**The Seduction of Jason** #21 Fayrene Preston	$1.95
☐	21623	**Breakfast In Bed** #22 Sandra Brown	$1.95
☐	21624	**Taking Savannah** #23 Becky Combs	$1.95
☐	21625	**The Reluctant Lark** #24 Iris Johansen	$1.95

Prices and availability subject to change without notice.

Buy them at your local bookstore or use this handy coupon for ordering:

Bantam Books, Inc., Dept. SW, 414 East Golf Road, Des Plaines, Ill. 60016

Please send me the books I have checked above. I am enclosing $_____ (please add $1.25 to cover postage and handling). Send check or money order—no cash or C.O.D.'s please.

Mr/Ms _____

Address _____

City/State _____ Zip_____

SW—12/84

Please allow four to six weeks for delivery. This offer expires 6/85.

LOVESWEPT

Love Stories you'll never forget by authors you'll always remember

LOVESWEPT

*Love Stories you'll never forget
by authors you'll always remember*

SPECIAL
MONEY SAVING
OFFER

Now you can have an up-to-date listing of Bantam's hundreds of titles plus take advantage of our unique and exciting bonus book offer. A special offer which gives you the opportunity to purchase a Bantam book for only 50¢. Here's how!

By ordering any five books at the regular price per order, you can also choose any other single book listed (up to a $4.95 value) for just 50¢. Some restrictions do apply, but for further details why not send for Bantam's listing of titles today!

Just send us your name and address plus 50¢ to defray the postage and handling costs.